THE DEVIL'S LEGION

Center Point
Large Print

Also by Jackson Cole and available from Center Point Large Print:

Six-Gun Stampede

**This Large Print Book carries the
Seal of Approval of N.A.V.H.**

THE DEVIL'S LEGION

Jackson Cole

CENTER POINT LARGE PRINT
THORNDIKE, MAINE

This Center Point Large Print edition
is published in the year 2023 by arrangement with
Golden West Inc.

Copyright © 1946 by Arcadia House Inc.

All rights reserved.

Originally published in the US by Arcadia House.

The text of this Large Print edition is unabridged.
In other aspects, this book may vary
from the original edition.
Printed in the United States of America
on permanent paper sourced using
environmentally responsible foresting methods.
Set in 16-point Times New Roman type.

ISBN 978-1-63808-632-1 (hardcover)
ISBN 978-1-63808-636-9 (paperback)

The Library of Congress has cataloged this record
under Library of Congress Control Number: 2022947581

THE DEVIL'S LEGION

ONE

"Don" Jose Muerta was a gallant figure riding at the head of his men as they swept eastward along the ancient Tornillo Trail. Clad in somber black velvet adorned with much silver, he sat his mighty black horse with the careless grace of a lifetime in the saddle. The gleaming pearl handles of his heavy guns flashed back the sunlight in opalescent sparkles, until his lean hips seemed belted with iridescent flame.

His riding gear was resplendent with silver, the bridle rein studded with Mexican opals, the bit rings burnished with gold. His stirrups were of solid silver, and plated with silver were his enormous, jingling spurs—spurs that never even tickled the glossy black flanks of the splendid black he rode; for to his horse alone, of all living things, was Jose Muerta gentle.

Jose Muerta was not really a don, although the blood of the hidalgos leavened the dark Yaqui flood that was predominant in his veins.

Jose Muerta's grandfather had been a grandee of Spain. His grandmother was an Indian princess, the daughter of a mighty Yaqui chief.

From his courtly grandfather Jose Muerta got his lance-straight figure, his fair complexion, and his hair that was like to the desert sands in the gold of sunrise. Only in his high cheekbones and his eagle-beak of a nose showed the Yaqui strain.

So much for the outer man. But the inner something that was the real Jose Muerta was the spirit incarnate of the proud, brave, ferocious and utterly cruel *Indios* of the mountains, who throughout the centuries that had passed since the Spaniard first set mailed foot upon the land that now was *Mejico* had never bowed in submission to the conqueror.

Yes, Jose Muerta was a gallant figure as he rode at the head of his more than a score of border raiders; but Lucifer must, too, have been a gallant figure as he led his cohorts from the mouth of Hell!

Don Jose glanced up at the sky—glanced with the eyes that were a heritage from neither his grandfather nor the Yaqui princess. Those eyes were peculiarly his own, and his most striking physical feature, large, palely blue, cold as steel, inhuman, remote, revealing nothing. They were the color of the water that flowed swift and silent in the shadow of the beetling ramparts of stone that upheld the towering crests of his native mountains. And in them was the silence, the inscrutable mystery, the unthinking, uncaring cruelty of the mountains and the cliffs and the rushing streams.

It was a stormy sky that met his gaze. The sun was sinking redly through fantastic cloud masses. The grim crags to the west were tipped with flame. Their mighty shoulders seemed to flow blood that seeped into a robe of fiery purple swathed about their breasts.

All about was an unnatural stillness that brooded over the rangeland that had been so bright and sparkling a few hours before, but now was blotched and painted with lurid shadows as the clouds cast their dark mantle, fold on fold, across the face of the setting sun. The hoof-beats of the horses rang unnaturally loud in that brooding stillness, and the jingle of the bridle irons and the popping of saddle leather jarred upon the ear. The horses themselves were nervous. They snorted, rolled questioning eyes, blew through flaring red nostrils.

Not far south of the Tornillo Trail began the desert that rolled onward to the distant Rio Grande and Mexico. The desert was fantastic and unreal in that dark sunset that brooded over the land. Chimney rocks started up like mis-placed tombstones. The cactus stood stiffly erect. Chollas, with needle-like spines, brandished weirdly deformed arms and seemed to writhe in torment under the red rays of the sunlight. The sands were stained a bloody hue, and in the utter silence of the waiting land, their eternal whis-pering was for the moment stilled.

It was a fit setting for the grim band that swept eastward along the old trail, eyes glinting in the shadow of low-drawn hatbrims, dark faces set like granite, sinewy hands never far from the weapons that swung at their hips.

Very faint and far away there rose a murmur that died, and rose again. It came once more, now a low mutter that quivered the still air. Then abruptly there was a rustling in the chaparral that fringed the trail on the north. It was a vast and stealthy rustling, as if an awakening giant were drowsily stretching his limbs amid the growth. A puff of wind tossed the manes of the speeding horses, died, came again, stronger than before. Lightning flickered on the western horizon, and there came a low, thudding murmur. Only the upper rim of the fiery sun was dimly visible through the shrouding cloud wreaths. It vanished. Great shadows climbed swiftly to the zenith. The fiery glow dulled to dusty rose, paled to a cold gray. The shadows thickened and the rangeland became vague and unreal.

And even the low mutter in the west increased in volume. A cold, steady wind fanned the cheeks of the horsemen. The west was now aflicker with bluish light. Like a blanket the darkness descended, blotting out the chaparral growth, the chimney rocks and the cactus. But the stealthy rustling continued as the unseen giant grew ever more restless.

The rustling grew as the giant stretched himself. He was fully awake now, and gathering his forces. Suddenly, with a bellow, he sprang into full life. An icy blast roared along the trail, then stabbing lances, then level sheets that whipped and stung. Overhead the black sky was slashed and forked and chained with vivid fire. The thunder mutter became a mighty rumble, a crackling crash. The air was full of broken twigs and flying leaves. The sands of the desert were no longer still. They hissed and whispered. They beat against the chimney rocks with a soft, grinding sound. They swirled amid the driving spears of rain. The lightning blazed. The thunder boomed. The mighty wind shrieked and bellowed.

"A wild night, *Capitan*," shouted Felipe, his lieutenant, to Jose Muerta.

"The better for our purpose," the bandit leader shouted back.

"*Si*," agreed the *teniente*, "but we have the many miles yet to go."

Like all the furies of Hell, the lightning blazed in the black sky, revealing fire-edged clouds that shot forth points and masses of vapor, thin like swords, or massed like charging horsemen. The thunder crashed, the giant wind howled and bellowed. The sheets of rain hissed through the blazing tumult. The hoofs of the speeding horses drove against the streaming surface of the trail, but with a silence as of ghosts. One whinnied, a thin, wavering thread of sound barely audible above the blare of the warring elements. Jose Muerta jerked up his head, his pale eyes peering into the darkness ahead.

Forth from the inky heavens burst a jagged, blinding flame that zigzagged downward in a torrent of fire. For a fleeting instant the plain ahead was as bright as a day of blazing sunshine.

Revealed in the dazzling flame of the lightning was a fork in the trail, a narrower track that turned sharply northward. And, crowding close against the chaparral that flanked the main trail, a tall horseman sat a great horse whose streaming coat shimmered molten gold in the bluish glare.

A crash of thunder that seemed to stun the very earth itself. The lightning vanished and blackest night rushed down.

Jose Muerta's voice rang out:

"*Desviar*!—turn aside!"

With instant obedience his men swerved to follow their leader along the stony track veering south.

"*Capitan*," Felipe shouted, "this is not the trail to Sanders. This leads back to *Mejico*!"

"Silence!" Muerta hissed, his voice snaking through the roar of the wind. "Did you not see that horseman at the forks? Who knows who he is, or why he was posted there?"

"But he was a lone man—we could have shot him," protested the *teniente*.

"Silence, fool!" Muerta repeated. "We *saw* but

a lone man. Who knows how many more might have been hidden in the growth at his back? It is because you do not think of these things that you are Felipe, and Felipe you will remain! Because I *do* think of them, I am Jose Muerta! Ride! I know this land. But a few miles further on is a trail that leads back to the Tornillo."

Sitting his great golden horse at the edge of the growth, Ranger Jim Hatfield stared into the darkness after the retreating hoofbeats of the shadowy band he had glimpsed in the lightning glare.

"Salty looking bunch of hombres," he mused. "Uh-huh, plumb cultus. Been up to no good, I'm willing to bet a hatful of pesos. But 'pear to be heading back to *manana* land. If they've been cuttin' a ruckus somewhere, I reckon I'll hear about it soon enough."

For some moments he sat gazing southward. But the lightning flashes revealed nothing of the vanished riders. No beat of horses' irons came to him on the wind. Finally he spoke to his great golden sorrel and rode on westward through the rain, toward distant Franklin and the Ranger post.

"Yeah, reckon they've headed back to Mexico," he repeated.

Which was exactly what Jose Muerta wanted him to think.

As Muerta had said, a few miles farther on the trail they were riding forked, one branch slanting sharply to the northeast. Into this fork Muerta led the way.

In due time they reached the Tornillo once more. Near midnight they made camp in the shelter of a cliff overhang. From their saddlebags they took food, which they cooked and ate. Then they lounged under the sheltering cliff, smoking cigarettes and talking in low tones. It wanted but an hour till dawn when they forked their horses once more and continued their eastward ride.

The rain had ceased, although the cloud masses still scurried before the wind. There were rifts in the clouds now, however, and the east was turning faintly gray. Muerta glanced at the paling sky, and quickened the pace.

Full morning had broken when Muerta and his raiders stormed into the little cattle shipping town of Sanders. They came yelling and shooting. The town marshal, an old man with a white beard, ran out of his office. Muerta shot him. The old peace officer never had a chance to go for his gun. He would have had scant chance had he held it in his hand before Muerta reached. A blurred flicker of a sinewy hand, a wisp of smoke and the marshal pitched forward on his face. Two other men who appeared on the street were coldly shot down.

The raiders, acting in perfect unison, took up posts at strategic points. In a matter of minutes the town was completely in their control.

Muerta, Felipe and several members of the band headed straight for the little bank building. They battered down the door and entered. There was swift, expert work on the door of the vault. The bandits backed to the front of the building, there was a muffled boom and the door crashed to the floor. Quickly the vault was rifled of its contents. A barked word of command, the dark-faced riders mounted, wheeled their horses and thundered out of town. Some daring individual who had secured a rifle sent ineffectual bullets whining after them as they vanished around a bend in the trail. The whole affair had covered a period of but a few minutes.

Many hours after the report of the Sanders outrage had buzzed over the telegraph wire to Franklin, Jim Hatfield rode in to Ranger headquarters. He found Captain Bill McDowell in a raging temper.

"The third raid that blankety-blank-blank has pulled off in less than three weeks!" stormed McDowell, "to say nothin' of a coupla big herds widelooped, and him shore for certain responsible. Hit Sanders with a dozen of his hellions, cleaned the bank of more'n ten thousand dollars—payrolls for the spreads and for that silver mine up in the hills."

"Come closer to being twenty of them than a dozen," Hatfield remarked quietly.

"Eh? Twenty! How the hell do *you* know?"

"Reckon I saw them on their way to Sanders," Hatfield replied, reaching for the makin's and proceeding to roll a cigarette with the slim fingers of his left hand.

Captain Bill's jaw dropped. He stared at his lieutenant and ace man.

"You—you saw them!" he stuttered at last.

"That's right," nodded Hatfield, "must have been them."

"But—but why didn't yuh do somethin' about it?" indignantly demanded the captain.

Hatfield shrugged his broad shoulders. "Because they put one over on me, that's all," he replied. "I met the hellions comin' lickety-split along the Tornillo Trail right at the forks thirty miles west of Sanders. A big lightning flash showed them up plain. At the forks they swerved into the south branch that heads straight for Mexico. Of co'hse I didn't know it was Muerta and his outfit. Didn't get more'n a glimpse of them in the lightning flash. I did figger it was an outfit what had been up to no good, but I also figgered they were headed back to *manana* land. Reckon Muerta saw me the same time I saw them. He's evidently a quick-trigger thinker. Took that south turn to make me figger he was headed for the river. I fell for it, and figgered just that, like he wanted me to. Then he musta cut back to the Tornillo by some track he knows about. Uh-huh, he put one over, all right."

"Wonder they didn't throw lead at yuh," grunted McDowell.

"Chances are they woulda, if they'd knowed for certain I was alone," Hatfield said. "Reckon they weren't sure about that and didn't want to get into a ruckus that they wouldn't gain anything by. Oh, that hellion has got plenty of wrinkles on his horns, all right."

"Yeah, he's smart, plumb smart," growled McDowell. "He put one over on *you,* and that ain't easy."

"But he put it over," Hatfield replied grimly.

As he made the remark, his long, black-lashed green eyes seemed to subtly change color until they were coldly gray as wind-swept winter ice. His rather wide mouth, ordinarily humorously grin-quirked at the corners, straightened to a hard line, and the whole aspect of his lean, deeply bronzed face was bleak as chiseled granite.

Captain Bill noticed the change, and under his mustache he murmured to himself:

"Uh-huh, yuh put one over, Muerta, but I've a hunch it was a damn costly put-over, as yuh'll find out before the last brand's run."

Aloud he said, "The big question is where will the hellion hit the next time? We gotta try and figger that, Jim, and be ready for him. Plenty of squawks comin' in about the way he's swaller-forkin' all over the section. One from the capital this mornin'. They wanta know over there what has happened to the Rangers."

Hatfield smoked thoughtfully for several minutes; abruptly he pinched out the cigarette butt and stood up, towering over the old captain, who was himself a broad-shouldered six-footer.

"Cap," he said, "if it's okay with you, I'm going to grab off a surroundin' of chuck, a cleanup and a mite of shuteye, and then I'm going to take a little ride over to Alamita."

"But, blazes, Jim, yuh don't figger Muerta will hit Alamita, do yuh? That's a county seat, and the biggest town in that county. Besides Salty Craig Wilson is sheriff there, and he's a tough hombre, and he hires deputies of the same sort as himself. Muerta ain't gonna take a chance on tanglin' with Craig Wilson, pertickler in a pueblo of that size. He's cultus, I know, but he ain't ever showed any signs of bein' plumb loco. Also, Muerta ain't never worked anything like that far east."

"All that's true," Hatfield admitted, "but I'll answer the last point yuh made fust. If yuh'll rec'lect, Muerta has been steadily workin' east all the time, just as if he was workin' on a definite plan. I've noticed that. Sanders is the farthest east he's ever got—forty miles east of his last strike before that."

"That's right," McDowell agreed.

"What yuh say about Alamita being a big town is so," Hatfield went on. "But it's the center of the richest cattle and minin' section anywhere's around. Also, it's known as a hangout for all sorts of shady hombres from both sides of the line. Muerta is mighty good at getting information on gold shipments, payroll times and cattle moves. I understand that Sanders's money was a big payroll sent in plumb secret, days before the usual time. I figger Alamita is a sorta clearing center for such things, and I've a plumb good notion Muerta has gents hanging out there that keep in touch with him all the time. By getting in touch with them is a way to get in touch with Muerta."

"That's right again," McDowell admitted.

"And as to Craig Wilson," Hatfield added. "What yuh say about him being a salty jigger is so, but all too often, it's been my experience, plumb salty jiggers are fast as to gun hand and slow as to thinking. I don't know, of co'hse, but Wilson may be that sort. Muerta has a fast gun hand, too—one of the fastest ever seen in this section, according to all reports, but he has something else that's just as hair-trigger fast—brains. That one he put over on me last night meant almighty quick thinking. Chances are Wilson and his men aren't anything like a match for him in that pertickler. So, everything considered, if it's agreeable to you, I'll take that little ride."

The old Ranger captain shrugged his shoulders,

tugged at his bristling mustache, and rumbled in his throat.

"All right," he agreed at length. "It's yore chore. Good luck!"

Hatfield smiled down at him from his great height, the quirking of his wide mouth suddenly making his stern face wonderfully pleasant.

"I've a notion I'll need it," he chuckled. "Not much doubt of Muerta being a cold proposition. So long, Cap."

Roaring Bill McDowell watched the Ranger's tall figure swing lithely out of the office. He nodded his grizzled head sagely.

"Uh-huh, Don Jose Muerta," he soliloquized, "I've a hefty workin' notion yuh plumb out-smarted yoreself this time. Uh-huh, yuh shore did, when yuh got the Lone Wolf on yore trail!"

TWO

Burning in a sky of silver-spangled black velvet, a red moon hung over the Coronado Hills. It was a bloody moon, sullen and menacing, low above the topmost crags that shot upward like snags of teeth in a festering jawbone. It seemed to glower upon the grim hills that glowered back in dark defiance yet flinching away from the lurid light that sought, in vain, to penetrate the ominous gorges where the cliffs overhung the moan and mutter of white water worrying the fangs of stone in the unplumbed depths. It was a moon fit to light the obscene orgies of witches and warlocks, of spectral elementals and goblins damned. Under such a moon, the Dawn Men, thewed like the aurochs and tusked like the great cave bear, must have howled loud to kith and kin to join them in the crimson feast, as in its sanguine beams they mumbled the bones of the slain.

Pouring into Lost Valley, battlemented east and west by the beetling cliffs of the Coronados, the light seemed to assume a quality of luminous shadow. In the lurid glow, spire and chimney rock appeared to crouch and shudder. The crooked branches of mesquite writhed as if in torment. Objects became distorted and unreal, deceptive as to bulk and distance, until the whole wide reach of the valley was as a raw and jagged wound made horrific by lumps and shreds of quivering flesh.

Suddenly the silence that brooded over hill and valley was broken by a singular deep throbbing that, rhythmic and solemn, shook the night air. Nerve-shaking and menacing, the deep beat rolled forth. It quickened, slowed, heightened into obvious question and answer. Far to the north broke forth a high staccato rattle, followed after a pause by a deep roll from the south. Then the beat resumed its throbbing monotony.

Riding the rimrock trail of the east wall of the valley, Jim Hatfield reined in his magnificent golden mount to listen. Motionless he sat for minutes, the concentration furrow deepening between his dark brows, while the air quivered to the ominous throb and mutter that, it seemed to him, monotonously repeated the syllables, "We will kill you, if we can! We will kill you, if we can!"

Over and over, the rumbling threat. "We will kill you, if we can!" said the men in the south. "We will kill you, if we can!" said the men in the north.

"Indian drums, Goldy, or I never heard one," Hatfield told his horse. "War drums, from the sound of them; but what in blazes does it mean? Geronimo and his Apache raiders just aren't any more, and there hasn't been any Indian trouble in this section for a mighty, mighty long time. This kinda stuff belongs to the old days. Drums! Talking drums. Sure wish I could read what they're saying. Is somebody trying to be funny?"

For a little longer the drums grumbled and muttered. Then the sound died away in a final long roll from the south, echoed by an answering whisper from the north. Again the eerie silence, broken only by the yipping, faint with distance, of a coyote, and a vicious reply from an owl nearby.

The tall rider shrugged his broad shoulders. He gathered up the reins, spoke to the horse. The clicking irons of the cayuse sounded abnormally loud in the stillness, and the popping of saddle leather was like muffled gunshots.

Then abruptly the silence that walled in the close, small sounds of the jogging horse was again broken. First there was a distant wisping clatter that grew to a mutter, a beat, a low thunder. Hatfield straightened in his saddle, stared down into the shadowy valley, from which the sound rose. Suddenly, a few hundred yards to the west, the straggle of chaparral birthed movement. From behind a jut of chimney rock bulged dimly seen shapes that rolled swiftly northward toward the distant mouth of the valley.

"Cows," the watcher muttered, "purty good-sized herd, too, and goin' like the wind. Now what in blazes does this mean?"

The herd flowed past his range of vision. Behind the galloping steers came mounted men—he counted seven altogether—flapping slickers, snapping quirts, lashing heaving brown backs with rope-ends. For a moment or two they loomed misshapen and huge in the reddish light, then they were gone behind a bristle of growth. The fading rumble of the speeding herd came back to the listener, lessened, died away.

But the silence did not at once resume sway.

Flung out of the south, like a misplaced echo of the drumming hoofs, came a stutter of shots, followed by evenly spaced reports, as if the unseen gunmen were carefully lining shots on a diminishing target.

Again Hatfield pulled up, staring ahead into the south. He shook his black head, listened intently. There was no sound of hoofs clattering toward him, no jingling of bridle iron swelling rhythmically out of the dark.

"Not headed this way," he muttered. "Figgered at fust that gun slingin' might have something to do with that herd larrupin' down this way, but I reckon not. Well, this is getting to be quite a night. June along, Goldy, and let's see what's next."

The "next" occurred with scant delay. Hatfield had ridden perhaps half a mile when his attention was attracted by a red glow slowly climbing up the southern sky and a little to the west. The moon, which had risen some distance above the mountain wall, had lost much of its bloody hue, and its light was changing to ashen silver that shimmered and softened the valley floor. But this new radiance was fierce and fiery.

The tall rider spoke to his horse and the animal quickened its gait.

"That's a house burning, or my name's not Hatfield," the rider declared. "Sift sand, yuh jughead, let's find out what's goin' on in this section."

The rimrock trail was plain and clear in the silvery moonlight now, and the golden horse flashed along like a shadow. His tall rider leaned forward in the saddle, peering intently at the widening and deepening glow. To his keen ears came faintly a sound of shouting. The trail curved, veered around a bulge of stone and an exciting scene met his gaze.

Directly ahead, the cliff which formed the east wall of the valley changed to a steep and boulder-strewn slope. Opposite this slope and perhaps a quarter of a mile out on the valley floor, a good-sized ranch house was burning fiercely. Flames were shooting from the roof and billowing from the lower windows. In the red light he could see figures running wildly about. Even as Hatfield reined his horse in and sat staring at the conflagration, several ran forward with a ladder which they placed against the wall so that its upper rungs rested on the ledge of a second story window. But directly beneath the upper window was a second window from which the red flames shot forth. They curled around the lower portion of the ladder, and when a man tried to mount it, he was driven back by their fierce heat. A second tried, only to fail. The figures retreated, shouting and gesturing.

The rider on the rimrock gathered up his reins once more. His lean, bronzed face, from behind the prominent high-bridged nose of which looked long, level, black-lashed eyes, grew stern and bleak, and the clear green of the eyes subtly changed until they were the pale color of a glacier lake.

"I figger we can make it down the slope, feller," he quietly told his horse. "Looks like somebody's in trouble down there, and no time to waste. Get goin'!"

The horse didn't like it, and said so with an explosive snort, but he took the slope, dancing down it on hoofs that were catlike in their sureness. Hatfield encouraged and steadied him with voice and hand. He reached the valley floor in a cloud of dust and a shower of displaced fragments, "settin' on his tail," skittered, reeled, all but lost his footing, but recovered his balance by a miracle of agility. Hatfield's voice rang out like a silver trumpet of sound:

"Trail, Goldy! Trail!"

Instantly the sorrel extended himself. He flashed

across the valley floor like the flicker of a cloud before a driving wind, eyes gleaming, nostrils flaring redly, hoofs thundering a drumroll of sound. Scant moments passed before he slithered to a halt in the yard of the burning ranch house.

Men shouted wildly and ducked for cover as the great sorrel crashed into their midst. Before he had plowed to a standstill, Hatfield was out of the saddle. His voice rang out, peremptory, edged with the authority of one absolutely sure of himself:

"What's goin' on here? Why yuh tryin' to get that ladder up?"

A babble of excited voices answered him:

"The Old Man! He's up there—second floor— saw him at the window—smoke got him—fell back before he could climb out—he's a goner!" were the comprehensible peaks above the clouds of whirling words.

Hatfield glanced at the window in question, from which at that moment the burned-in-two ladder fell with a clatter. He measured the distance with his eye. The flames bursting from the lower window were climbing the outer wall but were still below the second story. Back of the open window a reddish glow was beginning to strengthen.

"Fire eatin' through the floor," Hatfield muttered. "Stairs blocked. No tree close enough to climb up and swing in from."

He whirled and gripped by the shoulder a man who seemed somewhat less excited than the rest.

"Get me a crowbar or a posthole digger, even a spade with a long, strong handle," he ordered.

There was that in his voice which forbade question or argument. The man raced to a small outbuilding nearby and returned, a moment later, with a long-handled spade.

A glance told Hatfield that the stout handle was of seasoned hickory and capable of withstanding great strain. In the meantime he had untied his rope from his saddle and removed his cased guitar. He noosed the spade handle in the middle, took a turn and a hitch and drew it tight. Then he flung the spade up and poised it over his shoulder.

For an instant he stood rigid, like a bronze statue of a javelin thrower. Then his long right arm shot forward. The spade hurtled through the air, kept straight by its heavy metal head, the rope trailing behind. Right through the open second-story window it shot, to land on the floor with a clatter that sounded above the roar of the flames.

"If that thing hit the Old Man in the head, he needn't go to the trouble of gettin' hisself burned up," somebody declared.

Hatfield drew the dangling rope taut, whipping the sag up before the flames from the lower window could sear it. As he had expected, the long handle of the spade caught on either side of the window frame and held fast.

Instantly the trained roping horse tightened the rope and threw his weight back against it until it hummed in the air. Hatfield gripped the taut line with sinewy fingers and went up it hand over hand.

A roar of protest went up from the assembled cowboys. "Feller, yuh'll get caught up there and roasted, too," one yelled.

"The fire'll burn the rope through and yuh can't git back!" another bellowed.

"The Old Man's suffocated by now, anyhow," a third declared. "Don't try it, feller."

He could hear Goldy snorting, the scrape of his slipping hoofs, but he was confident the sorrel could withstand the strain, and he knew he would never slacken the rope until he received the word to do so. Now he was dangling over the flame-spouting window. Its furnace breath seared his flesh. He gasped in the fiery, smoke-laden air. For an instant his brain whirled, his senses reeled. Then he gripped the window ledge, drew himself up and with a plunge and heave sprawled on the floor.

The room was thick with smoke, baking with heat. Near the far wall flames flickered through the floor. Hatfield could hear their ominous roar and crackle outside the closed door. The door itself creaked and groaned under the beat of the draft rushing up from the furnace below. Once let it give under the strain, and a volcano of fire would pour into the room.

For a moment he lay gasping in the clearer air near the floor. Then he raised himself to hands and knees and began groping about. An eternity of frantic search and his hands encountered a limp body. He felt of the man's heart and found it beating feebly.

"Mebbe we'll make it yet, feller," he muttered. He whipped the stout kerchief from about his neck, found the man's wrists and bound them firmly together. Then he stood up, gasping in the heat, and looped the bound arms about his neck. The man was a heavy burden, but he was inches shorter than Hatfield's much more than six feet. With Hatfield standing erect, he dangled by his bound arms.

Awkwardly Hatfield shuffled to the window. Gripping his unwieldy burden with one arm, he inched onto the sill until he was in a sitting position, his legs dangling down the wall, his boots crisping in the heat that beat up from the flames that were so close they licked the soles. Then he gripped the rope with both hands and slipped off the ledge.

"If yuh slip or take a step now, it's the big jump, feller," he muttered, apropos of the golden horse.

But Goldy didn't slip. He snorted loudly as the double weight strained the rope. Irons gripping the ground, legs widespread and stiff as bars of steel, he reared back and stood rigid. The cinch creaked, the saddle tree popped and groaned. But the stout hull stayed together and the girth held.

Burdened as he was, Hatfield could make but slow progress down the sagging rope. It seemed to him that for an age he hung over the blistering flames, his lungs bursting for air, his arms aching with the strain that every instant threatened to tear his hands from their grip and hurl him and his helpless burden into the furnace beneath. The slant of the rope was not enough to permit him to slide down. His progress had to be hand over hand as he had ascended. The onlookers watched grimly.

He passed out of reach of the flames, glanced down. The ground was still a long way off. To let go now meant a broken leg, at the least, for himself; possibly a broken neck for the unconscious man. Grimly he struggled on. His muscles were trembling, his hands felt as if a red-hot iron were being passed back and forth across the palms. His heart sounded like an over-pressured engine, the blood roared in his veins. There was an ever-tightening band around his chest, suffocating him, sapping his strength. Dimly he could hear the sound of excited shouts somewhere far, far below. Then suddenly he felt hands gripping his legs. With a gasp of relief he let go his hold and in an instant was sprawling on the ground in a tangle of overthrown cowboys.

But the rescuing hands broke his fall. He felt the strangling arms of the unconscious man plucked from around his neck, the heavy drag of his body removed. Hands lifted him to a sitting position. Somebody pressed the uncorked neck of a bottle to his lips.

"Son," a voice declared, "you and the Old Man are both livin' on borrered time!"

THREE

With the stimulus of the drink, Hatfield's head quickly cleared. Assisted by friendly hands, he stood up. Behind him sounded a protesting snort.

"Ease off, Goldy," he flung over his shoulder to the horse.

"Don't need to," said the man who had spoken. "Rope just burned through and fell down. Son, that was the goldurnest smartest piece of work I ever seed. How in blazes did yuh come to think of it?"

Hatfield smiled down at him from his great height, his even teeth flashing startlingly white in his bronzed face, which was suddenly amazingly pleasant.

"Dunno," he admitted. "Figgered I had to get in that window somehow, and haven't sprouted wings yet. Calc'lated a rope was the only way to do it by. Rec'lected how I used to flip a rope with a rock tied onto the end up into a tree when I was a kid, when the trunk was too big to climb and the fust branch too high to reach. Reckon that gave me the notion. It worked."

"It shore did," said the other, "and the Old Man has got it to thank for not wakin' up with a coal shovel in his hands. How is he?" he called to the cowboys who were ministering to the unconscious man.

"Comin' out of it," came the reply. "Be settin' up cussin' in another minute."

The questioner held out his hand. "Son, my name's Blakely—Tom Blakely," he said. "I'm foreman of this spread, the YJ, and the old man yuh saved is the owner, Cal Higborn."

"My name's Hatfield—fust handle whittled down to Jim," the other replied. They shook hands gravely.

"But what's all this about?" Hatfield asked. "How'd the fire catch?"

Blakely let loose a string of cracking oaths. "Didn't ketch," he growled. "Was sot—sot in half a dozen places to once, on the fust floor. Fire arrow or somethin' shot onto the roof, too. When we heerd the noise and tumbled out of the bunkhouse, she was blazin' all over. We throwed lead at a coupla sidewinders hightailin' it away from here, but I reckon we didn't mark up no hits."

"Was set," Hatfield repeated. "Who set it?"

Blakely swore some more, and shook his fist at the shadowy south.

"By them blankety-blank Injuns, who else!" he declared.

"Indians? Yuh mean there's Indians raidin' up from Mexico?"

Blakely shook his head. "They live down there at the head of the valley," he replied. "Allus lived there, I reckon. Claim to own the land.

34

Everythin's contrary wise in this blankety-blank section. Injuns ownin' land! The head of this blasted valley is where the mouth oughta be! The land slopes to the head instead of to the mouth. Shore the Injuns sot it. The other day we caught one of the blankety-blank bucks snoopin' around on our spread and give him a prime hidin'. This is their way of gettin' even."

"Fellers taking the law in their own hands usually make for trouble," Hatfield remarked quietly. "Got any real proof the Indians set this fire?"

"Nope," Blakely admitted reluctantly. "Yuh never can prove anythin' on a Injun. The Old Man had a row with old Chief Mukwarrah over some unbranded stock a few months back, and there's been trouble hereabouts ever since. Plenty of stock has been widelooped."

"Any proof the Indians widelooped the stock?" Hatfield asked.

"There I gotcha!" Blakely replied triumphantly. "Nobody seed 'em do it, and lived to tell about it. Nobody found the beefs. But the only way yuh can run lifted steers outa this valley is by way of the south. There ain't a place, east or west, yuh can run 'em up through the hills. And there's a town at the south of the valley, and it would be plumb impossible to get a herd past it without it bein' spotted. Rustled cows would hafta go south, and across the Injun range. Which means the Injuns musta lifted 'em, or in cahoots with whoever did. See?"

"Sounds reasonable," Hatfield was forced to admit, "but still yuh haven't got proof that would stand up in a co'ht of law."

"It won't hafta stand up in a co'ht, before we're done with the hellions," Blakely promised grimly. "Say," he exclaimed suddenly. "I'll betcha while yuh was ridin' this way yuh heerd drums! Did yuh?"

Hatfield nodded.

"I knowed it!" Blakely exulted. "Every time they cook up some deviltry, they beat those blankety-blank drums. They was heerd early the night the Block A lost cows. And when the Walkin' Y lost part of their shippin' herd, they beat the night before. And when Baldy Yates of the Camp Kettle was drygulched, the damn things beat the very same night just after dark. Baldy musta been shot just about sunset, we figgered. That's prime proof the Injuns set this burnin', if yuh heerd the drums."

Hatfield nodded thoughtfully, and refrained from further comment.

Just then a sputter of cusswords told that old Cal Higborn had regained his senses. A few minutes later the YJ owner got to his feet and hobbled over to profanely thank Hatfield.

Higborn proved to be a stocky, bristle-whiskered oldster pointedly at variance with his lanky, clean-shaven foreman. With an old border campaigner's efficiency, he immediately took charge of the situation and began evolving order out of chaos.

"The ranch house is a goner," he growled, glaring with truculent blue eyes at the flame-spouting structure. "Lucky there's plenty of sleepin' room in the bunkhouse. There's some Dutch ovens and an old range in the stable. Better set 'em up to cook on. See the storehouse didn't ketch. So we don't go short on chuck. Plenty of pots and pans in there, too. We'll hafta sorta camp out till we can build a new *casa*. We'll start on that soon as the ashes cool on them foundations. Ain't this one helluva note, anyhow!"

The punchers went to work, setting up an improvised kitchen in the front part of the big barn, where there was plenty of room. By the time they had gotten everything necessary done, the fire was well on the way to burning itself out. While the work was going on, Hatfield and a couple of others kept a sharp watch on the roofs of the barn and other outbuildings on the chance that a stray brand might fire them also. Fortunately, however, there was little wind, and the danger decreased as the fire burned lower.

"Well, I reckon that's all we can do tonight," Higborn announced at length. "Figger we might as well try and grab a mite of shuteye 'fore come mawnin'. Things 'pear to be quietin' down."

But they weren't. As the tired workers headed for the bunkhouse, a clatter of hoofs sounded on the night air, growing swiftly louder. The men turned to stare southward in the direction of the sound. The hoofs drummed still louder, and a sweat-lathered horse flashed into the circle of the firelight. On his back was a wild-eyed cowboy who rocked and reeled in the hull. His face was stiff with caked blood and he appeared in the last stages of exhaustion.

"It's Harley Bell!" someone yelled. "What the hell's the matter with you, Harley? What happened?"

The injured hand was helped from his saddle and steadied on his feet. He stared dazedly at the still burning ruin of the ranch house. Under repeated urging, he found his tongue.

"The shippin' herd we was gettin' t'gether," he mumbled. "She's gone—widelooped. Purdy's dead—head bashed in. Musta hit me a glancin' blow—I ain't dead—yet."

"What in blazes are yuh gabbin' about, anyhow?" bellowed old Cal. "Shake yoreself t'gether and tell us what happened."

"Hellions slipped up on me and Purdy," Bell managed to reply. "We was ridin' herd; met under a tree while makin' our rounds. Stopped for a brain tablet t'gether. Tree set on edge of brush. Dark, with a damn red moon seemin' to make it darker. I heerd Purdy grunt, and as I turned to

38

see what was the matter, somethin' hit me over the head. When I come to, the herd was gone. I found Purdy layin' on the ground with his hoss standin' beside him. Hull back of his head was caved in. Managed to fork my bronk and ride here. Happened not long after dark. What time is it now?"

"Way past midnight," somebody replied.

"Hellions got hours and hours start, then," Bell mumbled.

"And before we could get after them, they'll be out through the head of the valley and well on the way to *manana* land," Higborn remarked grimly. "Take Bell in and wash his head and plaster it. Nothin' we can do t'night."

Again the cowboys headed for the bunkhouse, chattering angrily about the latest outrage, and profanely blaming the Indians at the head of the valley.

But Jim Hatfield, recalling a shadowy herd of cattle fleeing madly through the red light of a bloody moon, was silent, and the concentration furrow was once more deep between his black brows.

"Funny," he told Goldy, as he gave the sorrel a final once-over. "Looks like we're sorta off-trailin' the chore we set out to do; but, hoss, I got a hunch. We'll just stick around this section for a spell."

FOUR

The following morning found the YJ cowboys early astir. After quantities of steaming coffee, and a hot breakfast the cook threw together on the old range in the barn, several rode out to bring in the body of Purdy, the slain puncher. Old Cal Higborn called Hatfield aside.

"Yuh got the look of a top hand about yuh, son," he said. "I lost a good rider last night and that leaves me one short. There's a job open here if yuh'd care to sign on, that is if yuh're figgerin' on hangin' around in this section for a spell and ain't just passin' through."

"Notion I will hang around for a spell," Hatfield replied thoughtfully. "Reckon yuh've hired a hand."

"Fine!" applauded Higborn. "I'm ridin' to town now to let the sheriff know what has happened. Yuh can ride with me and sorta look the range over on the way."

A wrangler brought the horses around, and Hatfield and the owner set out.

"It's four hours' good ridin'," Higborn remarked. "We'd oughta make it in by noon; but don't go lettin' that yaller hellion of yores out. I've a notion there ain't many cayuses that can stay nose to nose with him if he's really in a hurry."

40

"Old Goldy can step a mite if he takes a notion," Hatfield admitted. "Say, this is a sorta nice looking range."

"It's a good one, when things are runnin' smooth," Higborn replied. "Good grass, plenty of water. Canyons in the hills that pervide shelter from sun and snow. With the right sort of neighbors, yuh're sorta settin' purty, but so long as them damn Injuns hold control of the head of the valley—"

He trailed off into profane rumblings. Hatfield, gazing across the emerald billows of the grassland dotted with thickets and groves and walled east and west by tall cliffs, was silent and thoughtful. He noted, and recalled Blakely's remark of the night before, that the general slope of the land was toward the head of the valley rather than toward its mouth. Which was unusual. The hill-locked valley was unusual in other ways. He estimated its width at some thirty miles, the western cliffs being hazy with distance. The trail they were following, he noticed, veered steadily to the west in its northward trend.

"Section looks like it all of a sudden dropped down hundreds of feet some time a million years or so back," he mused. "Uh-huh, got all the appearance of a sudden subsidence. Even after ages of erosion, those cliffs are still torn and ragged. No signs of a big stream ever having run here to cut the valley down through the hills.

Wonder just what did bring it about? Volcanic eruption to the east or west, perhaps, draining off some great reservoir and undermining the hull section, causing the land to sink."

Hatfield, before the murder of his father by wideloopers and the subsequent loss of the elder Hatfield's prosperous ranch set him to riding the dim trails that border the land of outlawry, had had three years in a famous college of engineering. He was interested in geological formations. In the years that followed the interruption of his collegiate career, he had kept up his studies after a fashion and, while he was not a certificated engineer, he knew more about the subject than many a man who could write a degree after his name. This unusual valley interested him very much.

He was recalled to the present by old Cal's rumbling voice. Higborn was veering his horse into a track that cut the main trail at a sharp angle. They had been riding some two hours and had doubtless covered about half the distance to the town at the valley mouth.

"Over west a mite more'n a mile is the Block A ranch house," said Higborn. "I wanta stop and see Blaine Ollendorf a minute. Blaine owns the spread and is a purty good feller."

As they rode into the yard of the ranch house, a man came out onto the porch to greet them.

"Hi, Blaine," shouted Higborn. "Want a word with yuh."

Ollendorf was a big, massively built man with abnormally long and thick arms. His features were bold and well-marked, with a mane of tawny hair sweeping back from his broad brow and curling low at the back of his square head. There were dark rings below his black eyes, however, and the eyes themselves were bloodshot, Hatfield noted, the lids slightly puffed.

"What brings yuh down this way so early, Cal?" he asked as they climbed the steps.

"Headin' for town to see the sheriff," Higborn replied. "Wanta come along?"

Ollendorf shook his head. "Was to town yesterday," he said. "Got back just about dark and went right to bed. Was plumb tuckered out. Got up just a while ago. Wanta ride up to my south range soon as I've had a bite to eat. Join me in a helpin'?"

"We et early," Higborn replied. "I'll tell yuh what happened over to my place last night."

He regaled the Block A owner with a vividly profane account of the previous night's occurrences. Ollendorf clucked sympathetically, shaking his square head as the tale progressed.

"And if it hadn't been for Hatfield here, I wouldn't be tellin' yuh about it," concluded Higborn. "I was sound asleep in my room upstairs when the shootin' outside woke me up. I was all groggy with smoke. The room was full of it. I managed to get to the door and open it. Fire was roaring up the stairs and along the hall. Had sense enough to shut the door, but that was about all. Tried to get to the window. Couldn't breathe. Couldn't see. Felt myself goin'. Never did get to the window. Next thing I knowed, I was layin' on the ground with the boys workin' over me. They told me what Hatfield had done, just like I told you. Yeah, I owe him plenty. Want yuh to know him. Shake hands with Blaine Ollendorf, Hatfield."

Ollendorf glanced keenly at the Lone Wolf, an inscrutable look in his black eyes, as they shook hands.

"Plumb glad to know yuh," he acknowledged heartily. "I'd have felt mighty bad if anythin' had happened to Cal. Mighty lucky yuh happened along so handy. Yuh say yuh're ridin' in to see Sheriff Fanshaw?" he asked Higborn.

"Uh-huh. And if Willis don't do somethin' about it pronto, I've a mighty good notion to take my boys and ride to the head of the valley and chase them damn Injuns clear to Mexico, I shore have."

Ollendorf shook his head in disapproval. "I wouldn't do that if I was you, Cal," he counseled. "After all, yuh got no real proof old Mukwarrah and his bucks fired yore ranch house and run off yore herd. Suspectin' ain't provin', yuh know, and yuh'll find yoreself up against the law if yuh try to run them Injuns off the land they own."

"What right they got to own land?" bellowed Higborn.

"The co'ht over to the capital says they own it fair and square," Ollendorf pointed out. "Yuh know what happened when Baldy Yates tried to make out that land was part of the Camp Kettle spread. The co'hts said the old Spanish grant by which Mukwarrah got his title was plumb valid, and they upheld Mukwarrah's side of the arg'fyin'."

"Uh-huh, but if Baldy hadn't been drygulched and left with a slug through his head right after he started the suit, he'd have won out," declared the stubborn Higborn. "Baldy was smart and salty, and he'd have found a way. Mukwarrah knowed that, and that's why he had Baldy drygulched."

"No proof that Mukwarrah had anythin' to do with it," demurred Ollendorf. "Baldy was plumb salty, as yuh say, and there was plenty of fellers who had it in for him. He had trouble over in the west rincon of the Big Bend before he came here; folks over in that section are sorta good at holdin' grudges."

Jim Hatfield took no part in this conversation. He sat perched on the porch railing, swinging one long leg, his eyes fixed thoughtfully on the rusty iron boot scraper nailed to the end of the lowest step, apparently paying no mind to what was being said.

"Just the same, if somethin' ain't done pronto, I'm ridin' to visit Mukwarrah," finished Higborn. "And," he added grimly, "I won't have no trouble with the law afterwards, 'cause there won't be no witnesses agin' me. I've stood just about all I'm gonna stand."

"By the way," said Ollendorf, changing the subject, "do yuh need lumber to rebuild with? I got a coupla stacks yuh can have. Had quite a lot of feet left when I finished my new barns. It'll save yuh a haul from Concho."

"That's just what I wanted to see yuh about," admitted Higborn. "It's mighty nice of yuh, Blaine. I'll send the wagons over t'morrer. Be seein' yuh."

Ollendorf nodded good-bye to Hatfield as they turned to go. "Drop in any time yuh're ridin' hereabouts," he invited.

"Blaine's a mighty accommodatin' feller, even if he is loco in the head where them damn Injuns is concerned," remarked old Cal as they rode back to the main trail.

Hatfield nodded, but refrained from further comment.

The day had turned hot, and they rode more slowly than before their visit to the ranch house. An hour passed and they had covered somewhat less than the remaining distance to Concho, the shipping town at the mouth of the valley. The trail had been constantly veering westward and now they were but a slight distance from the precipitous slopes of the east wall.

The garrulous Higborn kept up a constant chatter and was heedless of his surroundings, but Hatfield, on the other hand, spoke seldom and, when he did, in monosyllables, while his keen eyes searched every thicket and jut of chimney rock that they passed, and continually probed the thick growth on the slope to their left. During his years of riding furtive trails, Jim Hatfield had learned to be watchful, particularly in a section where there were inexplicable happenings. And now, in some corner of his brain, a silent monitor was setting up a clamor that all was not well. Hatfield had learned to heed that unheard but very real voice and had before now profited from not disregarding its warnings.

Higborn was grumbling something anent the misdoings of the Indians of Lost Valley. Abruptly his growling monotone changed to a yelp of surprise and anger as a long arm swept him from the saddle and crashing to the ground. Almost before he landed, Hatfield was beside him, crouched low, his heavy Winchester in his hands. The long barrel flung up, and lined with a puff of smoke which at that instant wisped from the growth some distance up the slope.

Even as a bullet yelled through the air over the

startled horses' backs, Higborn saw Hatfield's eyes glance along the sights. Fire spurted from the black muzzle of the saddle gun. The crash of the report was an echo to the one slamming down from the slope.

The growth on the slope was violently agitated for a moment, then was still. The silence was unbroken. There was no further evidence of movement in the veiling brush.

"Keep down," Hatfield's voice warned. "If I just winged him and he's still able to fang, we'll hear from him again if he manages to line with us. I've a notion we're out of sight in the grass."

For long moments they lay rigid, eyes fixed on the growth. Hatfield measured with his eyes the distance to a straggle of thicket that grew on the valley floor at the base of the slope.

"I've a notion I can make it," he muttered. "If I can, I'd oughta be able to creep up the slope and mebbe get in back of the sidewinder, if he's still there. Wuth a try, anyhow."

With the words he was on his feet, crouching low, zigzagging to the thicket at a swift run. But even as he dived into its shelter, a figure crashed into the brush alongside of him.

"Think I'm gonna hole up there like a gopher while you make a try for the hyderphobia skunk?" old Cal demanded indignantly. "I was a scout and doin' border fightin' afore you was born. We're in this t'gether."

"Okay," Hatfield chuckled, smiling down at the flushed face of the angry oldtimer. "Take it easy, now, and don't make a noise. If he's still up there and locates us, we're liable for a dose of lead poisoning before we can line sights with him. Let's go."

He quickly realized, however, that old Cal could move through the brush as silently as himself. Slowly and cautiously they wormed their way up the slope until Hatfield decided they were slightly higher than the spot from where the shot had come. Then they diagonaled to the south with even greater care.

Abruptly Hatfield laid a restraining hand on his companion's arm. Only a few yards distant was something huddled beneath a bush. They crept toward it, but the form remained motionless. A moment later they were standing over it, guns ready. But still there was neither sound nor movement.

"Done in, all right," Hatfield said.

"Shore is," Higborn agreed, jerking his thumb toward the black hole between the dead man's staring eyes. "Yuh drilled him dead center, son. How in blazes did yuh come to see him?"

"Saw the sunlight glint on his rifle barrel when he shifted it," Hatfield replied. "Had a notion that slope might bear a mite of watching. It's perfect for a drygulchin' of anybody riding the trail down there."

Old Cal peered at the face of the dead dry-gulcher, uncertainly seen in the shadow. Suddenly he swore an exultant oath.

"What'd I tell yuh?" he barked. "Look—it's a Injun, one of old Mukwarrah's Yaqui bucks, shore as yuh're a foot high!"

Hatfield squatted beside the dead man, examining the swarthy distorted face with calculating eyes. The drygulcher was undoubtedly an Indian. He was very dark, almost black, with a broad, evil looking face. His mouth was a wide slit, his nose flaring-nostriled and fleshy. He wore his straight black hair in a bang across his low forehead.

Hatfield turned to the chortling Higborn. "Yuh say Mukwarrah and his bucks are Yaquis?" he asked.

"Uh-huh," replied Higborn, "every one of 'em. Come up from *Mejico* originally. Ornery mountain Yaquis, that's what they are. This is the time we got it on the hellions. They can't worm out of this one. Caught with the smooth-iron hot!"

Hatfield was staring curiously at the dead man's lank hair. Now he turned again to Higborn, and straightened up.

"Cal," he said, "I don't like to mention it, but last night I sorta did yuh a mite of a favor."

"Yuh shore did," old Cal agreed emphatically.

"Well," said Hatfield, "I'd sorta like to ask yuh to do me one in turn."

"I promise even afore yuh ask," Higborn instantly rejoined. "Anythin' yuh ask. Half my spread, if yuh want it."

"Wouldn't know what to do with it if I had it," Hatfield smiled. "What I want yuh to promise is not to say anything to anybody about what happened here this morning, until I give the word."

Old Cal stared at him in bewilderment. "I shore don't know what yuh're drivin' at," he sputtered, "and it sounds plumb loco to me, but I've passed my word, and I ain't never bruk it yet."

"Okay," Hatfield accepted. "Let's see what this hellion has in his pockets. Might tell us something about him."

The contents of the dead man's pockets held no significance, however. Hatfield did not appear surprised or disappointed.

"His horse had oughta be somewhere around," he commented. "Mebbe we can find it."

After considerable search, they located the horse tethered in a dense thicket. It was a shaggy-coated, unkempt animal, unshod and unbranded. The rig was plain and bore no trademark.

Again Hatfield did not appear surprised. Without comment he got the trappings off the animal and turned it loose to graze.

"Can take care of itself, I figger," he told Higborn. "About half wild as it is. Chances are it'll take up with some wild herd in the hills.

Had oughta be plenty of that sort hereabouts."

"There are," agreed Higborn. "Gonna leave this feller lie?"

"For the present, anyhow," Hatfield replied.

"Reckon the buzzards will take care of him," Higborn predicted cheerfully.

"Yes," Hatfield agreed with peculiar emphasis, "I expect the buzzards *will* take care of him."

Higborn grunted agreement again. He did not overhear Hatfield's murmured remark to his horse:

"Feller, the hunch is workin'!"

FIVE

The interview with Sheriff Willis Fanshaw in Concho proved to be a rather stormy one. Higborn stated his grievances and demanded justice. Sheriff Fanshaw was willing to oblige, but didn't see his way clear just how to go about it.

"I'll get a posse t'gether and comb the hills for yore cows," he told the rancher, "but I can't go ridin' to Mukwarrah and accuse him of liftin' 'em, not without proof."

"Helluva lot of chance yuh'd have of findin' 'em now," Higborn replied caustically. "Them cows are plumb to Mexico, and you know it. If yuh don't do somethin' pronto, I'm gonna do some ridin' myself," he added pointedly.

The sheriff flushed and tugged at his mustache. "Takin' the law in yore own hands won't get yuh anythin', Cal," he replied.

After leaving the sheriff's office, Hatfield and Higborn repaired to a saloon for a drink and a s'roundin' of chuck. While they were eating, two men entered and approached their table. Higborn greeted them as old acquaintances, and introduced Hatfield.

"This is Andy Ballou of the Walkin' F, and Thankful Yates, who owns the Camp Kettle," he announced. "Thankful come over from Arizona and took charge after his brother, Baldy Yates, was drygulched. Yuh heerd me speak to Blaine Ollendorf about Baldy this mawnin', Hatfield."

Andy Ballou was corpulent and cheerful. Yates was tall and thin. He had a hard face, a tight mouth, and calculating gray eyes. He packed two guns, and his movements were lithe and furtive. With a single swift, appraising glance he took in the broad-shouldered, lean-waisted Ranger from head to foot. His gaze lingered a moment on the two heavy black guns hung low in carefully oiled and worked cut-out holsters from double cartridge belts, then quickly shifted away. His handshake was firm and cordial.

Ballou exclaimed and swore as old Cal outlined his misfortunes of the night before. Yates, evidently a taciturn individual, offered no comment other than a nod of his red head. Both invited Hatfield to drop in if he happened to ride in the neighborhood of their ranch house.

"Thankful is the black sheep of the Yates family, I reckon," Higborn observed as they headed back for the YJ. "Baldy was just sorta gray-colored. Thankful got inter a shootin' down in the Big Bend a few years back and hadda light out till things cooled down. Was in Arizona when Baldy got killed. Came back to take over the Camp Kettle. Seemed sorta sobered and has behaved hisself since he was here. He's pizen with them two guns, though, I'm told."

Hatfield went to work for the YJ, and quickly won the approval of both Blakely, the foreman, and the hands. Soon Blakely assigned him to the difficult and ofttimes dangerous work of combing strays from the brakes and canyons of the west range, which was work to Hatfield's liking, giving him, as it did, ample time for some apparently incomprehensible investigations of his own. He spent much time in the gorges and canyons, examining them in the minutest detail.

One afternoon, beyond the south limits of the YJ range, he was riding slowly along not far from the west wall of the valley. He was about to push through a final fringe of thicket he had been traversing when his eye was caught by something going on some distance ahead. Reining Goldy in before he had left the concealment of the thicket, he lounged in the saddle and watched curiously the activities of a group of men who sat their horses under a large tree. Hatfield counted eight altogether.

"Now what in blazes are those jiggers up to?" he wondered.

As he watched, the men wheeled their horses and rode swiftly toward the western slope, all but one, who remained sitting his horse under the tree.

Hatfield followed the group with his eyes until they had vanished into the brush of the slope.

Then his gaze returned to the single horseman, who still sat stiffly erect in the shade of the tree. His horse stood motionless, save for an occasional impatient stamp of a hoof or a switch of his tail to drive away the flies.

"Is that jigger posing for a picture, or something?" Hatfield mused. "Hasn't moved an inch since the others left."

His curiosity thoroughly aroused, he spoke to Goldy and rode slowly toward the motionless man, casting an occasional glance toward the slope which had swallowed up his companions.

Still the man did not move. He sat lance-straight on his horse, staring straight ahead of him, his hands apparently resting on the pommel of the saddle.

Slowly Hatfield approached. As he drew nearer, he could make out what looked like a thin black line running from the man's head to a branch of the tree. A little nearer, and suddenly he stiffened in the saddle.

"Blazes!" he muttered. "Of all the hellish things to do!"

He swore under his breath as he realized the fiendishness of the thing. It was a veritable refinement of cruelty.

The black line was a rope. One end was noosed about the man's neck. The other was fastened to the tree branch overhead. Hatfield could now see that his hands were bound in front of him. He was all set for a hangin', and hanged he would be, despite the departure of his executioners.

For the horse was not tied. Let it take a step forward and the man would be dragged from the saddle and left dangling by his neck. There he must sit, awaiting with nerves tortured to exquisite agony the inevitable happening. He might be able to keep the horse still with his voice for a while, but sooner or later the animal, driven by hunger or thirst or some wayward impulse, was bound to move.

Hatfield was in a quandary. Any minute the horse might move. If he approached slowly, he might well be too far off, should the horse take a step, to reach the victim in time to save him. If he urged Goldy to speed, his approach might frighten the animal and cause it to run. After a swift mental calculation of the risks, he resolved on the former course as the safest.

Step by step the golden horse moved forward. Hatfield could see the forward pricking ears of the other animal as it focused its gaze on the approaching sorrel. It stamped nervously, tossed its head. The helpless man's lips moved. He was doubtless talking to his mount in low tones, endeavoring to allay its nervousness.

Hatfield was still several hundred yards distant. The horse under the tree was evincing more and more nervousness. Once it moved a little, and the dangling rope tightened. The man strained his head back to ease the pressure on his throat. His helpless fingers twitched spasmodically. Hatfield could see his chest heave as he fought for air.

Step by slow step. Hatfield's face was bleak as the granite of the glowering cliffs. His eyes were cold as water torturing under frozen snow. One slender hand dropped to the black butt of the gun nearest it.

The horse was plainly frightened by the slow advance. Hatfield felt Goldy shiver as its nervousness was communicated to him. It raised a forefoot, stamped, twitched its tail, tossed its head. And still a hundred yards to go. The horse snorted, blowing prodigiously through its flaring nostrils. Hatfield saw its muscles tensed. And fifty yards yet to go!

The frightened horse snorted again. It plunged forward, went careening off across the range. Its rider was jerked from the saddle and left dangling in mid-air, his body writhing, his legs kicking convulsively.

Instantly Hatfield's hand flashed down and up. Clamped tight against his sinewy hip, the long black gun spouted flame. The reports blended in a veritable drumroll of sound as the Lone Wolf pulled trigger.

Swiftly he counted the shots. "One—two—three—four—five!" The Colt rock-steady, he hesitated an instant, squeezed the trigger. He gave a gasp of relief as the writhing body suddenly dropped through the air and thudded on the ground. The severed end of the rope snapped sharply up amid the branches. Hatfield's voice rang out:

"Trail, Goldy! Trail!"

The great sorrel shot forward with the speed of light. Hatfield went out of the saddle with him going at full gallop. Leaning far back on his heels, he kept his balance. He dropped beside the prostrate man and with frantic fingers ripped the tight noose from his swollen neck. His face was black with congested blood, the veins on his forehead standing out big as cords.

But his heart was still going, his lungs working. Gasping and retching, he fought for breath. The blood drained from his face, his lids fluttered. A moment later they raised, and steady black eyes stared up into Hatfield's face.

The man was an Indian. Hatfield saw that at a glance. His face was aquiline and finely featured, though it was a network of wrinkles. His hair, hanging in a straight bang across his broad and high forehead, was white as driven snow. His mouth was well formed and kindly.

"Take it easy, oldtimer," Hatfield cautioned. "Get yore breath back and rest a mite. Yuh came mighty nigh to makin' the Happy Huntin' Grounds that time."

The old man lay motionless for a few minutes, without speaking, his unwinking black eyes still regarding the face of his rescuer. Then, with the assistance of Hatfield's arm, he raised himself to a sitting position and spoke:

"Mukwarrah thanks you!"

SIX

Squatting comfortably on his heels, Hatfield rolled a cigarette with the slim fingers of his left hand and proffered it to the old chief. Mukwarrah accepted with a nod. Hatfield rolled another for himself and they smoked silently, Hatfield's eyes constantly searching the western slope the while. Mukwarrah read his thoughts with native shrewdness.

"I do not think they will return," he remarked.

"Mebbe not," Hatfield admitted, "but no use taking chances." He rose, slid his Winchester from the saddle boot and laid it on the grass beside him.

"They might," he remarked hopefully.

"It will be greatly to their misfortune if they risk themselves within range of the Lone Wolf's guns," Mukwarrah commented.

Hatfield shot him a swift glance. "How come yuh know me?" he asked.

"Many know you," the chief returned imperturbably. "Especially those who are lowly or in need of help. You could be no other. I know none but *El Lobo Solo* could have shot as you shot when you severed the rope and saved my life."

With a smile, Hatfield changed the subject. "Yuh talk mighty good English, Chief," he observed.

61

Mukwarrah nodded. "I was educated in the San Vicente mission across the Rio Grande," he explained.

"Yuh do talk English more like an educated Mexican than a Texan," Hatfield agreed.

The old chief stood up, still slightly unsteady on his feet. Hatfield followed the direction of his glance.

"I'll fetch yore horse for yuh," he offered. "I see he's got over his scare and is grazing over there by the slope."

He caught the horse with little difficulty, and Mukwarrah mounted.

"Will you visit my village?" he invited.

Hatfield considered a moment, glancing at the sun.

"We can reach the village before it is dark," Mukwarrah said.

"Okay," Hatfield agreed.

As they rode down the valley, Hatfield asked a question:

"How'd those hellions manage to tie onto yuh?"

"They roped me as I rode near the slope," Mukwarrah explained. "It was cleverly done. I was helpless before I could raise a hand."

"Recognize any of 'em?"

"They wore masks over their faces," the Yaqui replied.

Hatfield nodded. "Happen to get a look at their hands?" he asked casually.

Mukwarrah shot him a quick glance. "The hands of three were dark," he replied.

Again Hatfield nodded. "And I reckon it was them three that figgered out that cute little hangin' trick," he observed. "They're good at that sort of thing."

Mukwarrah nodded grave agreement.

The sun was setting when they reached the site of the village, and in the light of its level rays, Hatfield could see, in the far distance, the narrow gorge that led to the Rio Grande and Mexico.

The village, a group of well-built lodges, was set on a little mesa rising considerably above the valley floor. Good crops were growing on cleared land and the range was dotted with grazing cattle. Hatfield saw numbers of horses and mules, and a fine herd of goats.

"We are peaceful folk here," Mukwarrah observed. "All we ask is to live in peace with our neighbors, and so we did until recently. Now we constantly fear trouble. The *Senor* Higborn, and others, think ill of us. He thinks we rustle his cattle."

"I've a notion he'll get over that 'fore long," Hatfield replied quietly.

"I hope so," Mukwarrah said. "The charge is most untrue. My young men do not steal. I have reared them in the faith of the good fathers of the mission. They obey the laws of their land, for it *is* their land, as it is the land of the *Senor* Higborn and his friends. They would fight and die for it if necessary."

"Yes," Hatfield agreed with warmth, "I've a plumb notion they would. And I've another notion—that the time will come when Higborn and his friends will sit in yore lodge as yore friends."

The old chief gave him a long look. "If *El Lobo Solo* says it is so, then it *is* so," he remarked simply.

After a bountiful supper in the chief's lodge, Mukwarrah proposed that the young men put on a tribal dance for their guest's edification. Hatfield knew that the Indian, contrary to popular opinion, was not a solemn and taciturn individual. Here was laughter and gaiety and sociability. He enjoyed the dance greatly, knowing he was witnessing a spectacle it is given to few white men to witness. It was past midnight when the jollification broke up and Hatfield went to sleep in the chief's lodge.

"Mukwarrah," he said the following morning as he stood beside his saddled horse, "Mukwarrah, is there any other way out of this valley besides across yore range or by the town in the mouth?"

"Not that I have ever heard of," the chief replied. "Not that it is impossible that there is one. So far as I know, there has never been a need for another, so why should anybody look for one?"

When Hatfield reached the YJ ranch house, in the late afternoon, the place was in an uproar.

"A big herd shoved off the Walkin' Y spread last night," Higborn told him.

"And them damn Injun drums was beatin' again," Tom Blakely added. "I tell yuh, boss, we gotta do somethin'. I'm scairt to death about our shippin' herd we're gettin' t'gether. I can't keep the boys out there guardin' all the holdin' spots every night, but as shore as we don't, them hellions is gonna run a bunch off. We can't afford to lose any more cows."

"We'll do somethin'," Higborn promised grimly, "and mighty soon."

A little later he drew Hatfield aside. "By the way, where was yuh last night?"

"Down in Chief Mukwarrah's village," Hatfield replied.

Old Cal's jaw dropped, his eyes goggled. "For Pete's sake, don't let anybody else know about it!" he sputtered. "If folks find out yuh was with them Injuns when Ballou's herd was widelooped, they'll—"

"Higborn," Hatfield interrupted, "that widelooped herd never went across Mukwarrah's range."

Old Cal stared. "Then where the—" he began, but Hatfield interrupted again.

"Mukwarrah's bucks put on a tribal dance for me last night," he told the rancher. "The shindig lasted until long past midnight. It was bright starlight in the early evening, with a bright moon later on. No herd coulda gone through the gorge and not been seen. All of Mukwarrah's young men were there when the dance busted up, and they were all there early this morning when I left. Yuh'll hafta leave Mukwarrah out of this one, anyhow."

"If you say that, I reckon I'll hafta," Higborn admitted. "But if the Injuns didn't do it, who did?"

"That remains to be found out," Hatfield replied quietly. "I'm going to pound my ear for a spell. I wanta ride over to the west range early tomorrow."

He was riding the range very early the following morning. Before daybreak, in fact. The level rays of the rising sun found him close to the western wall of the valley, riding very slowly northward along the base of the cliffs, his keen gaze intently searching the ground.

Mile after mile he rode, and found nothing. Then, some miles north of the confines of the YJ range, where the overflow of a little spring formed a patch of marshy ground, he came upon a multitude of hoof marks. Here and there, also, were the imprints of horses' irons.

"Might be just a bunch stopping here for a drink," he mused, scanning the scored ground, "but those prints are deep, and splayed out.

Looks more like a herd siftin' sand almighty fast. Headed north, too, and the prints don't look very old."

He rode on, intent and watchful, but the thickly growing grass of the rangeland was impervious to the marks of passing hoofs. Only once his quick glance noted something encouraging. It was a fresh white score on a slab of rock, the kind of scrape made by the slipping iron of a shod horse.

Several miles more, and in the cliff wall yawned the dark mouth of a narrow canyon. The floor was hard and stony, thinly grown with brush except along the walls, where it was thick and tall, but there were signs that cattle had from time to time entered the gorge.

"Not that it means much," Hatfield muttered. "Chances are there's water back in here, and the steers would nacherly go for that. Still, some of those marks look fresh."

He turned into the canyon, which slashed the hills in a westerly direction. Soon he discovered that there *was* water in the gorge—a good-sized spring that gushed from under the rock wall and formed a stream which ran into the depths of the canyon.

Hatfield's eyes glowed with interest. "Sorta proves my theory about the geological formation of this section, anyhow," he told himself. "The slope of this canyon is away from the valley, not toward it. I figgered I'd find something like this sooner or later."

With quickened interest he rode on, following the banks of the little stream. He had covered perhaps three miles when the stream began to broaden and overflow its banks. Soon Goldy was splashing through a small marsh of sticky black mud grown with rank grasses. Hatfield's eyes glowed again as they rested on the dark surface of the bog.

And the marshy ground was slashed and scored by a multitude of hoofprints.

"Fresh, too," he exulted. "Not more'n forty-eight hours old."

The prints led into the gloomy depths of the canyon. Hatfield followed them, Goldy's hoofs sucking and splashing in the black mud. The stream continued to broaden and shallow. Finally the water vanished altogether, absorbed by the spongy ground, sinking to unknown depths, doubtless to drain off by way of some subterranean channel. The ground began to grow more firm, the bog stiffened, and a little farther on was replaced by hard, stony soil upon which the hoofs of the passing herd left no imprint. For perhaps a mile farther Hatfield rode, then he abruptly reined Goldy in and sat staring. He swore under his breath with bitter disappointment.

Directly ahead was a sheer rock wall towering

up against the blue of the morning sky. The canyon was a box.

"Looks sorta like the nice little house we built is all tumbled down, feller," he told the horse. "A goat couldn't get up that rock, and the side walls all the way in are just as steep. Begins to 'pear that in here is just a watering spot for stray dogies."

He rolled a cigarette, lighted it, and sat frowning at the blank wall.

"Just the same, those hoof marks back there didn't look like the prints of strayin' cows," he growled. "Looked a heap more like they were made by a herd being shoved along hard and fast. Has somebody found a way to sprout wings on beefs, or lizard legs? 'Pears sorta like it."

With a disgusted snort, he turned Goldy's head, veered him toward the south wall of the canyon and rode slowly back the way he had come, examining the rock wall for some cleft or fissure he might have missed on his trip into the gorge, although he was confident that none existed.

The cliffs reared sheer, with a thick growth of chaparral at their base. Hatfield eyed the growth, searching for signs of the phantom herd brushing against it in passing, seeking some clue to their fantastic disappearance. The close bristle stretched unbroken as the rock wall towering above it.

Abruptly he reined in, his eyes narrowing. His

searching gaze had noted a subtle difference in the stretch of growth he was just passing. It stood straight and tall, but there was a withered look about the leaves on the topmost branches, a tinge of yellowishness at variance with the fresh green on either side. For perhaps a dozen feet this peculiar manifestation was evident.

His eyes glowing with excitement, Hatfield slipped from the saddle. Through his mind was running recollection of stories of owlhoot tricks told by old border peace officers. He approached the growth, broke off a branch of one of the bushes. It snapped sharply in his fingers.

"Dry!" he muttered. "Dead and dry!"

He stooped, seized the gnarled trunk with both hands and tugged sharply. Instead of resisting his efforts, the trunk slid easily out of the ground. It had no roots. Its base was a sharpened stake!

Hatfield tossed the bush aside, seized hold of another. A moment of tugging and he had a gap in the growth a couple of yards in width. Through it shone the cliff wall, and in the wall yawned a dark opening!

SEVEN

Wordless, Hatfield stared at the cave mouth. Then he shoved his wide hat back on his crisp black hair and gave a low whistle.

"An old trick!" he exclaimed aloud, "but a good one! Cut out the brush, then stick it back in the ground after yuh pass through the gap. That way there's no broken branches or tramped down bush. Anybody ridin' through here would never suspect that cave in the cliff. Would never notice the break in the growth unless they were looking mighty sharp and had a good notion what they were looking for. Wouldn't have noticed it myself if those hellions hadn't got careless and neglected to replace the withered bushes with fresh ones. That's the way with the owlhoot breed—allus overlooking some mite of a thing. Not much, a few withered leaves, but enough to make a jigger stretch rope. Goldy, I'll bet yuh a hatful of pesos that cave is a tunnel that runs right straight through the hill and inter a gorge or valley on the far side. And in that gorge will be a trail leading south. Let's you and me go and see. Wait a minute, though. It's dark in there, and the going is apt to be rough."

He searched about amid the growth until he found some pieces of dry resinous wood.

Lighting one for a torch, he led Goldy to the mouth of the cave.

The sides of the cave were smooth and water-worn, its floor carpeted with fine silt sprinkled with pebbles and small, rounded boulders. Hatfield nodded with satisfaction.

"Just what I figgered we'd oughta find sooner or later," he remarked. "A waterway through the hills. Uh-huh, that's the old bed of a stream that once ran through here, a mighty long, long time back, when this section was different from what it is now. And look at the hoof marks in that silt! Plenty of cows been shoved through this hole."

He mounted, and rode into the cave, holding his torch high. Goldy's irons clattered loudly on the boulders, but the floor had a slight slope and was devoid of pitfalls. For perhaps a mile Hatfield rode through thick darkness relieved only by the flickering flame of his torch. Then suddenly he saw light ahead. Five minutes more and he was sitting his horse in the far mouth of the tunnel. Before him stretched a narrow gorge that trended in a southerly direction. And down the middle of the gorge ran a trail that showed evidence of recent travel.

"Uh-huh," he nodded with satisfaction. "This is their private back door to *manana* land and a market for widelooped beefs."

With a final glance at the gorge, which flowed

southward for as far as his eye could reach, he turned back into the tunnel. Reaching the canyon once more, he carefully replaced the cut brush, making sure that all was as before. Then he rode swiftly to the canyon mouth and headed for the YJ ranch house.

Old Cal was working at his desk when Hatfield entered. He looked up, glowering from under his bushy brows.

"Now what?" he demanded. "Somethin' else bust loose?"

Hatfield drew up a chair. He was fumbling at a cunningly contrived secret pocket in his broad leather belt. He laid an object on the desk between them.

Cal Higborn stared, his jaw sagging. The object was a *silver star set on a silver circle,* the honored, feared and respected badge of the Texas Rangers!

"A—a Ranger!" stuttered the old rancher. "Yuh—yuh're a Ranger!"

"Figger to be," Hatfield smiled.

"And yuh're here to hawgtie them damn Injuns!" Higborn exulted.

"I'm here to try and hawgtie the gents who have been doing the widelooping and general hell raising in this section," Hatfield corrected with emphasis. He slid the silver badge back into its secret pocket.

"Remember, if folks in general hereabouts

73

know me to be a Ranger, my value to the outfit would be cut down quite a mite," he cautioned.

Higborn nodded his appreciation of the fact. "What yuh aim to do?" he asked.

"Cal," Hatfield replied with a question of his own, "yuh got two holdin' herds all ready to join tomorrow and shove to the shipping pens in town, one on yore north range, and one on yore south. Right?"

"That's right," Higborn agreed.

"Figgering as yuh do, that yore beefs have been rustled through the south end of the valley, which herd will yuh guard careful tonight?"

"The herd on the south range, of co'hse," Higborn replied instantly.

"Right," Hatfield nodded. "With that herd well-guarded and the boys all on the job, nobody could run the north herd past them, either. That way both herds would be safe. There's good grass and water on the north range where the herd is, and yuh'd know the beefs wouldn't do much strayin' during the night. Yuh'd figger to pick 'em up easy when yuh start yore drive to the pens in the morning. And I've a hunch," he added with meaning, "that some other gents are gonna figger all that out just like I'm telling yuh. I figger they won't be able to resist that big herd of fat beefs wuth a heap of dinero. While yuh're keeping yore eyes skun on yore south herd, they'll be plumb busy shovin' the other herd down Mexico way, without a chance, or so they figger, of having a loop dropped on them."

"But how in blazes—" Higborn began.

"I'll tell yuh," Hatfield interrupted. Briefly he outlined what he had discovered in the hills.

"Been looking for just some such thing," he explained. "I figgered fust off, from the geological formation of this valley, that there should be some old waterways through the hills, nacherly .by way of one of the canyons. Mebbe a million years back, this section was different. The floor of this valley was considerable higher than it is now, which means that the side canyons sloped out of the valley instead of into it. Water must have run through those canyons to the west and south in those days. Then came a mighty big and sudden subsidence and the valley floor sank to where it is now. Most of the old waterways got closed up since then, but I figgered mebbe one might still be in existence. There is, and by way of that, cows have been run out of this valley."

"How in blazes did yuh figger it out?"

"The night I rode inter this section, I saw a herd being pushed along mighty fast—to the *north*. I figgered at the time it looked sorta funny. Then when Harley Bell rode in with his head busted and told about the widelooping, I was plumb sure the herd I saw was yores. I was, as I said, headed north. That's what started me thinking of another way out of this valley. Now let's get busy. Have all the boys ride out to the south holding spot before dark. Those hellions will be keeping a sharp watch on what's going on. Then, after it is good and dark, we'll slip the boys away, all except a couple we'll leave to keep the fires going and make it look like everybody is on the job at the south holding spot. The rest of us will snuk inter that canyon and see what happens. I'm willing to bet a hatful of pesos that before come daylight tomorrow, there won't be any more rustling to worry about in Lost Valley."

"But if the Injuns ain't doin' it, who is?" demanded old Cal as he stood up and buckled on his gun.

"I've got a purty good notion, but I'm not saying until I'm plumb sure," Hatfield replied. "We'll know before morning."

Where the cut brush hid the mouth of the cave, the canyon was dark and silent, with a silence broken only by the mournful sighing of the wind in the leaves. Nothing moved amid the shadows. There was no sign of life.

Then, faint with distance, sounded the wailing bawl of a tired and disgusted steer. The querulous bleats drew nearer, were undertoned by the low rumble of many hoofs. Moving shadows loomed in the starlight. There was a creaking of saddle leather, a jingle of bit irons as men dismounted and began removing the cut brush.

Suddenly light flickered, burst into a dazzling glare as oil-soaked brush flamed fiercely. The red light beat on the faces of the YJ cowboys, standing grim and ready, guns out. It beat on the faces of the amazed rustlers, and on the square Prussian head and livid face of Blaine Ollendorf, standing a little to one side of his men, directing the movements.

In the tense hush, Jim Hatfield's voice rang out, edged with steel:

"Yuh're caught settin'! Don't reach! Get yore hands up!"

With a yell of fear and fury, Ollendorf went for his gun. Hatfield shot him before it cleared leather. He reeled, pitched forward onto his face, writhed over on his back and lay twitching. The canyon rocked and bellowed with a roar of six-shooters.

It was all over in a minute. Caught wholly by surprise, the demoralized wideloopers didn't have a chance. Almost instantly four of their number were stretched on the ground. The others threw down their guns and howled for mercy.

"Tie 'em up," Hatfield ordered tersely. He closely scrutinized the faces of the owlhoots. His eyes showed bitter disappointment.

"Not here," he muttered. "And I'd figgered he would be. Looks like my hunch wasn't so good, after all. Let's see what I can learn."

He knelt beside the dying Ollendorf, who glared up at him with hate-filled eyes.

"*Verdamnt* Ranger!" he hissed through his blood-frothing lips. "Ha! soon your kind will be but a memory!"

"Ollendorf," Hatfield said, "where is Jose Muerta?"

The Prussian's eyes bulged.

"You—you know!" he gasped.

"I know you were just one of Muerta's hired hands, you and yore Apache bucks," Hatfield told him quietly. "Where can I find Muerta?"

Ollendorf stared at him, his eyes filming. He began to mutter, half in delirium:

"Der dream! der Great Dream. Ha! *Gotterdammerung!*"

" 'The Twilight of the Gods,' " Hatfield translated. "What are yuh talking about, Ollendorf?"

"Der Great Dream!" the dying man repeated. "Soon it will come true. There will be shouting, the tramp of armed men, the scream of der eagles! Ha! Gotterdammerung no more! The Old Gods will live again! There will be feasting and singing in Valhalla! *He* will make it come true— der Great Dreamer! Muerta? Ach, no! Not that tool der Great Dreamer shapes to his purpose. Jose Muerta? Ach! Der Great Dreamer. And der Dream! *Heil* Wotan!"

Ollendorf strove to rise, but fell back. Blood

poured from his mouth. He stiffened, and was still.

Jim Hatfield stood up and stared into the shadowy south.

"*Now* what have I stumbled onto?" he muttered. "The Great Dream! What did he mean by that? I followed a hunch, but now I've come to what I figgered to be trail end, I can't read the brand!"

The YJ punchers secured their prisoners, rounded up the recovered herd, and headed for home. Slightly in the rear, Hatfield rode with old Cal.

"I never woulda believed it of Blaine Ollendorf," said Higborn, shaking his head. "How come yuh to figger him in the fust place, Hatfield?"

"Didn't have much to go on, at fust," the Ranger admitted. "Just some mud on a boot scraper. Rec'lect the morning we rode up to his place. Ollendorf took good care to tell us he'd been in bed sleeping all night, and hadn't yet been out of the house. But there was black mud on his boots, and fresh black mud on the scraper. And his eyes had the look of a man who had been up all night and doing a heap of hard riding. I figgered the mud on the scraper must have come from Ollendorf's boots, and I couldn't help but wonder where he'd picked it up. Mostly red soil hereabouts, yuh know. And why should he lie about being out during the night? Looked funny.

Then when that hellion drygulched you and me by the slope, I did some hard thinking. Ollendorf was the only person we'd spoken to all morning, the only person, so far as I could see, who knew we were heading for town. Yuh'll rec'lect the trail makes a wide arc from his place, curving over west until it reaches the west slope. Straight across the range from Ollendorf's place would be the chord of that arc, and a heap shorter than around the curve. A jigger slipping away from Ollendorf's ranch house as soon as we were out of sight over the bulge could easy make it to the slope ahead of us, hole up and wait until we came along. Which, I figger, is just what happened. I caught a funny look in Ollendorf's eyes when he first saw me, a surprised look, and I figgered right off he'd recognized me as a Ranger. That was okay, but why should he be so anxious to put me out of the way in a hurry?"

"Because, knowin' about you and yore rep'tation, he figgered yuh were here to bust up his game," old Cal shrewdly deduced.

"Right," Hatfield agreed.

"But why did the hellion take up for the Injuns all the time? Looks like he woulda wanted to help make folks suspicious of them."

"Was smarter the other way. The nacherel thing for a guilty jigger to do was try to cast suspicion on somebody else. Ollendorf did the opposite, which really helped put him in the clear. I figger, though, that if things had showed up that proved Mukwarrah and his bucks couldn't be guilty, he would have managed in some smart way to get folks to looking sideways at Thankful Yates, who's sorta under a cloud."

"Why did yuh figger fust off the Injuns didn't have anythin' to do with it?"

Hatfield chuckled. "Fust off because of that drum beating you fellers made so much of, which was just another one of Ollendorf's tricks. Cal, I know something about Indian customs. About the only time they do any drum beating is when they are having a shindig, or when they're starting on the war path. Indians are just like the rest of us folks. If they have any skulduggery in mind, they don't go advertising it. You should know that, but I reckon yuh're like most folks who live next door to Indians, yuh never take the trouble to find out anything about them or their customs."

"I'm goin' to," Old Cal declared emphatically. "Come tomorrer, I'm ridin' down to Mukwarrah's place to eat a mite of crow. Reckon I plumb owe him a apology."

"Reckon yuh do," Hatfield agreed. "And I've a notion yuh'll get along prime with him. He's a fine old gent."

"What about that Injun who drygulched us? And we got three more of the same sort ridin' ahead there with their hands roped."

"That drygulchin' gent was an Apache breed,

with his share of white blood, which mebbe is what made him so ornery," Hatfield replied.

"How'd yuh know that?"

"Didn't have the look of a Yaqui, like yuh said Mukwarrah's tribe was. He'd cut his hair Yaqui style, but when he fell there with his head hanging over, there was a plain sign of a part on the left side. No Yaqui ever parts his hair. I knew right then that he couldn't belong to Mukwarrah's outfit, which tied up with what I was already thinking. Ollendorf slipped in a few breeds to ride with his wideloopers, so if anybody happened to get a look at the outfit operating, they'd figger fust off it was Mukwarrah's Indians."

"Wonder why they tried to hang old Mukwarrah, like yuh told me about?"

"Part of the scheme to set outfits against each other. That's an old owlhoot trick, and it usually works. Get a coupla outfits on the prod against each other, and pronto they blame each other for any skulduggery that's going on. Which makes it pie for the owlhoots. That's why they set yore ranch house afire, though that was possibly done, too, to distract attention from the widelooping the same night. That herd was sorta close to the ranch house when it was shoved off, wasn't it?"

"That's right. Yuh figger Ollendorf was responsible for Baldy Yates' drygulchin'?"

"Wouldn't be surprised. Mebbe Yates might have been smart enough to fenagle old Mukwarrah's land away from him. Ollendorf wouldn't want that to happen, of co'hse. Well, I reckon that's about all, and we're getting close to the spread. I crave a mite of shuteye. Wanta be gone in the morning afore the sheriff comes out rarin' and chargin' about folks who take the law in their own hands."

Old Cal gazed across the moonlit prairie and smiled complacently.

"Yeah, it's a plumb purty range," he said. "A fine place to live, with good neighbors livin' all around yuh. But I'll be almighty sorry to see you ride off, son."

"I've got an unfinished chore on my hands," Hatfield replied somberly. "I've a notion it's a long trail I'm riding. Mighty glad I stopped off here. Was able to lend some folks a hand, and I learned something that is liable to be mighty important—to Texas, and the country in general."

EIGHT

Alamita, roaring under the Texas stars, was a Helldorado equal to anything Dodge, Benton, or Hangtown ever had to offer. Three much traveled trails, including the rambling Tornillo and the Espantosa, which slithered northward from Mexico across the grim and weird fastnesses of the Big Bend, converged in Alamita. The Espantosa was a favorite with gentlemen who preferred to do their riding between the hours of sunset and sunrise.

Those latter found Alamita a tempting place at which to pause for diversion. Their pausing did not tend to elevate the moral standing of the community but was decidedly enlivening.

North and east of Alamita was splendid rangeland, where numerous beefs waxed fat and sleek on the rich needle and wheat grasses and the succulent curly mesquite. And these beefs were driven to Alamita for shipment. To the west were the Coronado mines scarring the grim battlements of the Coronado Hills. And from the Coronados came the silver ore that was ground to a watery paste in Alamita's stamp mills and resolved by the amalgam process to portly silver bricks, rich also in gold content. To the south was the Espantosa Desert, spired and chimney-rocked, where the sparse vegetation was the cactus in a myriad varieties, the greasewood and the sage.

The cowboys from the spreads to the north and east came to Alamita in search of liquid and other refreshment. The miners relaxed—if that be the right word for it—from their toil, in Alamita. Desert rats and prospectors from the south came to Alamita to renew their grub stakes and, incidentally, to wash the salt and alkali dust from their throats before again tackling the desert and its elusive promises of fabulous wealth. Chuck riders stopped over. Gentlemen whose antecedents would not bear inspection and whose futures were questionable favored Alamita with their presence.

Alamita welcomed them all, and it was a royal and hilarious welcome. Saloons, gambling hells, dance halls, and—other places—lined every street, particularly Chuckwalla Street, and all were open for and doing a roaring business.

As the lovely blue dust of the dusk sifted down from the Coronado Hills to the west and the windows changed from blank and staring eyes to squares and rectangles of gold, Alamita's low rumble of the afternoon crescendoed. From saloon and dancing hall came music, with bursts of song, or what was intended for it. The sprightly chink of bottle necks on glass rims mingled with the musical clink of gold pieces shoved across the green cloth. Roulette wheels whirred and clicked. Cards slithered one against the other with a seductive, silky sound. Dice skipped and rolled like spotty-eyed devils at play. There was a whirl and patter of words, bursts of laughter, sputters of profanity. The solid clump of boots punctuated the lively click of high heels on the dance floors. The vividly colored neckerchiefs of cowboys and the red, blue and plaid shirts of the miners formed a background for the whirl and shimmer of the scant costumes of the dance floor girls. On the great mirror blazing bars were long rows of bottles of every shape and color. The white coats and aprons of the barkeeps were strikingly in contrast to the somber black garb of the dealers at the gaming tables.

The whole scene was a kaleidoscope of color, changing, shifting, splashed with highlights, merged with shadows.

And as varied as the many hues were the faces of those who crowded the big rooms. Lean young cowhands rubbed shoulders with brawny hardrock men. Mexicans were present, garbed in black velvet resplendent with much silver. Bewhiskered desert rats in dusty shirts sat at tables, smoking thoughtfully, downing their drinks with monotonous regularity. Hard-faced, watchful men stood at the bars, drinking silently, and missing nothing of what went on around them. Lookouts sat on high stools, shotguns across their knees. Floor men sauntered about, keeping close tab on what was happening, ready for any emergency. The general atmosphere of most of the places was gay and lively, but with an undercurrent of tenseness that was never altogether absent. Alamita was a border town, and constantly prepared for the unexpected.

The most substantial building on Chuckwalla Street housed the Alamita bank. John Mosby was president of the bank. He was also owner of the Anytime saloon directly across the street, Alamita's second biggest.

Mosby was a grossly fat man with bright little blue eyes set deep in rolls of flesh. He had a big jaw, a bulbous nose and a well-shaped mouth about which there was always a cynically humorous expression. Despite his bulk he was fast on his feet and underneath his fat were long slabs of muscle. He wore an old Russian Model Smith & Wesson forty-four slung low on his right thigh, and he knew how to use it.

Mosby was also owner of the big Bar M ranch. It was said by some that he got his start in the cattle business by widelooping steers from the vast unbranded herds of the dons across the river; but that was a charge that had been brought against more than one prosperous cattleman. It was never specifically proved against Mosby. Mosby also owned a heavy interest in the Silver City mine up in the Coronados, one of the section's richest producers.

Most people agreed that the success of the

Alamita bank and the Silver City mine was chiefly due to Mosby's mine manager and bank assistant, Lynn Dawson.

Dawson was the antithesis, in appearance, of his elderly boss, and was some ten or fifteen years younger. He was tall and straight and well set up. He had a high-nosed, straight-featured face with a firm, hard mouth. His crisply curling hair was a light brown. His eyes were of a rather light shade of blue and were prominent; but they were seldom clearly seen by anybody because of the darkly colored heavy-lensed glasses Dawson habitually wore. For Dawson was almost blind. He wrote and figured with his nose little more than an inch from his work, and he walked slowly and gropingly, and always carried a cane with which he often tentatively tested the ground ahead as he walked along the Alamita streets. He rode well, and had the sense to trust his horse, so that when he was in the saddle his blindness was less of a handicap than might have been supposed. He dressed in somber black relieved only by the snowy front of his ruffled shirt and was excessively neat in his person and apparel. Nobody had ever seen him pack a gun, which, considering the condition of his eyes, was not remarkable.

"Sorta tied short as to eyesight but almighty long on brains," was the general consensus of opinion relative to Lynn Dawson.

Things were lively in the Anytime at midnight. The long bar was crowded, the roulette wheels spinning, the dance floor was thronged with jostling partners. Men sat silently at the poker tables, their conversation mostly restricted to grunts and an occasional growl of profanity.

John Mosby presided at the far end of the bar. Lynn Dawson sat alone at a small table, his eyes shadowy behind his thick lenses, sipping a glass of the best whiskey the Anytime could provide.

A sudden hush fell over the room as the swinging doors opened and a blocky old man entered and glanced about with cold, searching gray eyes. He had a square, deeply lined face and a bristling mustache. A well-worn cartridge belt encircled his bulky middle and from it swung a capable looking Colt in a hand-made holster. On his sagging vest he wore a battered silver badge, on which the engraved letters SHERIFF could scarcely be deciphered.

But Sheriff Craig Wilson could never be induced to trade in that scarred badge for a new one. Years before it had stopped a widelooper's bullet and saved the sheriff's life, which accounted for its battered appearance and Salty Craig Wilson's affection for it.

Behind Wilson sauntered a lanky, loose-jointed man with humorous brown eyes, hounddawg chops and a mouth that seemed constantly quirking upward at the corners. It was Skeeter

Ellis, the sheriff's chief deputy. Wilson looked hard, and was. Ellis looked mild and harmless, and wasn't.

Sheriff Wilson passed to the far end of the bar, after giving the room a careful once-over, and engaged John Mosby in conversation.

"I'll have a special guard up to the mine to bring that shipment in," he told the saloon owner. "I ain't takin' no chances with that."

"Ain't lookin' for or expectin' no trouble," replied Mosby in a high, squeaky voice ridiculously out of character with his ponderous bulk, "but mebbe yuh're right, Craig."

"Too much dinero rep'sented there to take any chances with," Wilson repeated. "Un'stand it's the biggest cleanup the Silver City has made yet."

"Reckon that's right," Mosby squeaked.

"What I can't ever un'stand is why yuh hadda go and build yore stamp mill up there at the mine, instead of packin' yore ore down here to stamp, where the bricks would be safe after they're melted down," the sheriff complained in querulous tones. His attitude was one of personal injury.

"Lynn Dawson talked me inter it, and I'm glad he did," returned Mosby. "Stampin' out the ore there at the mine instead of cartin' it way down here has saved me plenty dinero."

"And if there happens to be a raid on one of

them shipments what gets by with it some day, yuh'll lose plenty," growled the sheriff.

"We don't take much chances," Mosby pointed out. "Right now, for instance, nobody knows that shipment's comin' down tomorrow. Rec'lect, we had a guarded wagon roll down here yesterday and unload what was s'posed to be the shipment, only that them bricks unloaded were lead instead of silver."

"Yuh'll slip some time, see if yuh don't," grunted the sheriff, sucking the drops of whiskey from his mustache and calling for another drink.

Silence fell as he and Skeeter "appreciated" Mosby's good likker. Lynn Dawson got to his feet at that moment, groped toward the bar, said good night to Mosby and left the saloon. The din, which had abated somewhat at the sheriff's entrance, was in full swing once more.

Strikingly in contrast to the turmoil in Alamita was the silence and utter lack of activity at the Silver City mine, twenty miles to the west, high up in the Coronado Hills. The gaunt buildings that housed the stamp mill and other mining machinery were dark and deserted. A single light gleamed, in the watchman's shanty near the stamp mill.

In the shanty the watchman was bending over his little stove, throwing together his midnight meal, after the completion of his latest round.

Suddenly he raised his head and stood in an

attitude of listening. Outside, on the Tornillo Trail, which ran past the site of the mine, was the sound of a horse's irons, steadily drawing nearer.

Directly opposite the buildings the hoofbeats paused. The watchman stepped closer to where his rifle leaned against the wall. He picked up the long gun when he heard the crunch of boot soles on the gravel outside the shanty.

"Hello!" shouted a deep voice when the steps were some distance away. "Hello, inside. Any chance for a plumb hungry gent to grab off a helpin' of chuck?"

The watchman gave a grunt of relief and set down the rifle. There was something reassuring in the deep tones. He crossed to the door and flung it open. A moment later a tall, broad-shouldered man moved into the circle of light.

"Come on in, feller," the watchman called cordially. "Was just gettin' ready to set the table. Plenty in the pot for two."

"Fine," replied the newcomer. "I'll look after my horse fust, though."

"There's a shed in back of the shanty—oats in a bin, and hay," said the watchman. "Here, take my lantern, and hustle up. Grub's ready and I'm mighty sharp set."

The stranger took the lantern and vanished into the darkness. He reappeared a few minutes later, entered the shanty and shut the door. The watchman gave him a quick glance, noted that he had a lean hawk face, deeply bronzed, and dominated by a pair of long, black-lashed eyes of a peculiar shade of green. He wore the plain but efficient garb of the rangeland—faded blue overalls, soft blue shirt, batwing chaps, high-heeled boots of softly tanned leather, a broad-brimmed J.B. A wine-colored handkerchief was looped about his muscular throat. Double cartridge belts encircled his lean waist, and from hand-made cut-out holsters protruded the black butts of heavy guns.

The hospitable watchman nodded his grizzled head. "I'm Tom Welch," he announced.

"Hatfield's the name, fust handle Jim," the other supplied. "Glad to know yuh, Welch."

"Glad to have someone come along," Welch replied. "Gets sorta lonesome here on a night like this. All the boys are in town celebratin' pay day. Nobody around but me. Nobody else needed. The stamp mill won't walk away, and the monthly cleanup went to town yesterday, so there ain't really nothin' to watch. Mebbe we can have time for a little game of cribbage after we eat?" he added hopefully.

"Surest thing yuh know," Hatfield assured him. "Sorta hanker for company myself. Been ridin' for quite a spell."

"Cowboy, ain't yuh?" asked Welch, with a glance at the other's equipment.

"Sometimes, when I'm workin' at it," Hatfield

admitted. "Ridin' the chuck line right now."

"Ought not to have any trouble grabbin' off a good job hereabouts," the watchman remarked, evidently being familiar with the expression, "ridin' the chuck line." "Lots of good big ranches in this section, and I understand they need men."

He was removing a large pot of savory stew from the stove as he spoke. The table was already set for two, and a moment later they sat down together to an appetizing meal. A period of busy silence ensued, such as is customary with men showing their appreciation of good food. Finally Hatfield pushed back his plate and rolled a cigarette. The watchman fished out a black pipe and filled it with even blacker tobacco. They smoked thoughtfully for some minutes, with only a desultory remark or two passing between them. Then they cleared the table, cleaned up, and Welch produced a cribbage board and a well-thumbed deck of cards.

They played several games with practically even results. Welch abruptly glanced at his watch.

"Time for a round," he announced, "although there really ain't much sense of it on a night like this. Nobody around to drop a match or somethin' and start a fire, and that's about all I have to worry about, ordinarily. Yuh're a prime good cribbage player, Hatfield, and I've enjoyed it. I reckon yuh're purty tired after ridin' all day. I hafta stay up all night, and when I go off duty in the mornin' I'm headed for town to buy a few things I need. In that little back room is a comfortable bunk. You just pile in and get yourself some shuteye. Sleep as long as yuh want. Nobody will come in here to bother yuh. Hope I'll be seein' yuh again some time. We'll have another little game."

Hatfield shook hands with the hospitable watchman, and when the other had departed with his lantern, he removed his outer clothing and stretched out on the bunk, and was almost instantly asleep.

In men who ride much alone with danger as a constant saddle companion, there develops a subtle sixth sense that warns of menace when none, apparently, is at hand. This sense was highly developed in the Lone Wolf.

Abruptly he was wide awake, the silent monitor clamoring frantically in his mind, although there was no definable reason for its so doing. The night was deathly still, but he felt sure that some unexpected sound had awakened him. A light burned dimly in the outer room, but the watchman was nowhere in sight. Doubtless he was making one of his hourly rounds.

For minutes Hatfield lay listening. No sound broke the stillness. There was no movement detectable in or about the building. Then suddenly he heard a cry, a stifled cry that was cut off with knife-slash abruptness. He lay listening a moment longer. The cry was not repeated.

Hatfield swung his feet to the floor. Swiftly he slipped on a few clothes, and buckled his gun belts about his waist. As an afterthought he refrained from donning his boots. On silent feet he crossed the outer room, blowing out the light as he did so. He cautiously opened the door and slipped from the building.

The night was dark, for, although there was a full moon in the sky, its light was mostly obscured by a dense mass of black cloud.

Hatfield stood peering and listening. He heard nothing, and at first saw nothing. Then gradually he was aware of a faint glow of light seeping from the gaunt mill building. He was positive that the building had been totally dark when he turned off the Tornillo Trail some hours before.

Perhaps, though, he reasoned, it was but the light from the watchman's lantern. Welch might be inside the building, making a round. But the glow remained stationary and did not increase in intensity.

After a moment's hesitation Hatfield glided toward the building. A moment later he saw that the light seeped through an outer door that stood slightly ajar. Somebody was in the building, all right. He recalled the stifled cry. Perhaps Welch had fallen and hurt himself. He took another tentative step toward the mill, his keen ears caught a slight sound a little distance off, and instantly he hurled himself sideways.

In the midst of his instinctive movement, flame gushed out of the darkness to his left. The hills clanged echo to the crash of a gun. A bullet fanned Hatfield's face with its lethal breath.

"How in blazes did that hellion see to shoot so close in the dark?" was his surprised reaction as he whipped out his own guns and fired at the flash.

There was a second gush of fire. Another bullet screeched past Hatfield's ear. Still moving on his feet, he hurled himself sideways and down. And as he struck the ground, the black cloud slid past the face of the moon. Instantly a flood of silvery light made the scene as bright as day.

In the sudden blaze of ghostly radiance, Hatfield saw a tall man standing perhaps fifty feet distant. Behind him was a knot of riderless horses. Even as the Ranger stared, the man flung up his hand and jerked his broad hatbrim low, as if to conceal his face from the Lone Wolf's view.

But in that instant of vision, Hatfield saw a lean, high-nosed face with a hard mouth and glinting pale eyes. The man's head was turned slightly to the side, and in the moonlight his hair shimmered like molten gold.

"Jose Muerta, sure as hell!" Hatfield muttered as he pressed trigger.

But the outlaw was fast on his feet as he was

with a gun. He went backward and sideways like a leaping cat, his gun blazing fire.

In that instant of flooding moonlight, Hatfield had seen something else. Within two yards of where he lay was a pile of heavy timbers, neatly stacked. He dived for this shelter in a crouching scramble and hurled himself down behind its bulk.

The mill building was no longer silent. Inside sounded muffled shouts, and the pound of boots on the boards. Hatfield cautiously raised himself to peer over his shelter. He saw figures flitting out the door, that was now wide open. Both his guns let go with a rattling crash. He saw one of the figures whirl, stagger and plunge to the ground. The others, shooting and cursing, raced toward the plunging horses. The tall, golden-haired man had their bridles in his grip and was fighting to prevent their bolting.

Bullets pounded the timbers behind which the Lone Wolf crouched. Others grazing the tops of the beams, showered him with splinters. He ducked down again, stuffing fresh cartridges into his empty guns. As he ejected the last spent shell, he heard the drum of horses' irons. Without hesitation he stood up.

The outlaw band had mounted and was pounding westward along the trail. Hatfield sent slugs screaming after them; but a turn around a shoulder of rock hid them almost instantly. He stood listening a moment, while the click of racing hoofs faded into the distance. Then he cautiously approached the motionless figure sprawled before the mill door. The moonlight shone on a white, upturned face.

A single close glance showed Hatfield that the man was dead, a dark hole between his staring eyes. Without waiting to examine the body, the Lone Wolf slipped through the mill door, guns ready, and glanced about.

He was evidently in the mine office. By the light of a shaded bracket lamp he saw desks and tables scattered about. Across the room set in the wall, was a large steel vault, the outer and inner doors of which stood open. On the floor beside the vault were scattered several metal ingots of goodly size.

And to one side of the door by which he had just entered, his head rolling from side to side, groaning with returning consciousness, lay the sprawled form of Tom Welch, the watchman. Blood from his gashed scalp had formed a pool on the floor.

Hatfield knelt beside the injured watchman and explored his head with sensitive fingertips. He quickly decided that Welch was not badly hurt. His judgment was corroborated when the watchman opened his eyes and stared dazedly. A moment later he was sitting up, shaking his battered skull and sputtering profanity.

"What happened?" Hatfield asked.

"Damned if I know," mumbled Welch. "I saw a light in the office and come in to investigate. I stepped through the door, and that's the last I remember, exceptin' for a lot of stars and comets that went out plumb sudden."

"Somebody standing behind the door belted yuh over the head with a gun barrel, I reckon," Hatfield surmised.

"But what's it all about," Welch demanded, getting to his feet, a trifle shakily. He glared about the room. His eyes widened as they met the open vault and the metal blocks scattered on the floor. He weaved over to them, took a close look.

"Why, them's silver bricks," he explained. He peered into the open vault, where others were to be seen, stacked in orderly rows.

"It's the monthly cleanup, but how in hell can that be?" he exploded. "Day before yest'day I saw them bricks loaded inter a coach, with my own eyes!"

"Well, looks like somebody packed 'em back here," Hatfield replied, a trifle grimly. "And it looks like, too, that some other somebodies knew they were here, and tried to get 'em."

"And if it hadn't been for you, feller, they'd have got away with it," the watchman declared with conviction. "How come yuh happened along like yuh did?"

"Woke up and heard yuh yelp when they hit yuh," Hatfield replied.

"Uh-huh, I sorta rec'lect lettin' out a holler just as I went down. I was scairt."

"Don't blame yuh," Hatfield comforted. "Sorta unhingin' to get belted over the head when yuh're not expecting it. I think I did for one of the hellions. Let's go out and see. Bring yore lantern along. I see it isn't busted."

Outside, Hatfield carefully examined the dead man, turning out his pockets and giving his apparel a once-over.

The man, a scrawny individual with a peaked face, wore ordinary range clothes. His gun, which lay beside him, was of common make and caliber. His pockets discovered nothing of significance.

"His kind never carry anything to tie them up with somebody or something," the Ranger growled.

The man's hands interested him. They were long, well cared for, with thin, nervous looking fingers. Close examination convinced Hatfield that the tips of his fingers had been sandpapered.

"To make them over-sensitive," he explained to Welch. "Reckon this gent was the one who worked the vault combination. This kind isn't often met with in range country."

He recalled that a different procedure had been employed in the Sanders bank robbery. There the safe had been blown.

"Mebbe figgered they didn't have time to work the combination there," he mused. "Or mebbe that vault was equipped with a time lock, though that is sorta out of the ordinary in a section like this, pertickler in a small place like Sanders."

He stood up, took the lantern and walked to where he had seen the grouped horses. He examined the ground, and nodded.

"Thought I saw more horses than men," he remarked. "Reckon they brought along some spares to pack the stuff on when they got it out of the vault. Those bricks are sorta bulky, and weigh plenty. Chances are those spare cayuses were fitted with apparejos—pack saddles. Well, no use hightailin' after the hellions. They got a long start and they'll know how to hide their trail. Reckon we'd better head for town, come daylight, and notify the sheriff."

"That's right," Welch agreed. He drew out his bulky old silver watch and consulted it. "Nearly five o'clock," he said. "Some of the boys should be here by seven or a little after. We can turn the place over to them and ride to town. Figger there's any chance of those hellions comin' back?"

Hatfield shook his head. "Not them," he replied. "They'll figger we will be ready for them, and they won't know for sure how many of us may be around, after the surprise they got. Just leave everything as it is. The sheriff will want it that way."

"Then," said Welch, "I reckon we might as well go over to the shanty and cook some breakfast. I sorta feel in need of a mite of grub. I wanta tie my head up too."

Hatfield agreed and they headed for the shanty, the door of which stood open, yawning like a toothless mouth. Welch stumped across the room and lighted the lamp, which flared up smokily, casting a dim glow. He doused the lantern and started to trim the lamp wick.

And at that moment a voice spoke from the dark inner room:

"Hands up! And be quick about it!"

NINE

Jim Hatfield stiffened. For a fleeting instant he had a wild impulse to go for his guns, but sober sense told him it would be plain suicide to do so. The voice was soft, musical, but underlying the silky tones was a deadly threat.

"Caught settin'!" he grated between his teeth as he slowly raised his hands, shoulder high.

Welch had already "elevated," his hands high above his head, his jaw sagging.

A tall man stepped from the inner room. His hat was drawn low over his eyes. The lower portion of his face was muffled in a handkerchief. As the dim light from the lamp fell on him, Hatfield caught a glint of golden hair underneath his hat. In each hand he held a heavy pearl-handled gun, the black muzzles yawning at Welch and the Ranger. He gestured to Hatfield with his right-hand gun.

"All right, you," he said, his voice muffled in the folds of the handkerchief, "put your hands over your face, then move them down your middle, slow. Unbuckle your belts and let them fall to the floor. Steady, now, no funny business."

Hatfield obeyed. There was nothing else to do. His Colts thudded to the floor.

"Right," said the gunman. "Now kick them over into the corner. Right!"

He gestured to Welch. "I see you got laces in those high boots of yours," he said. "Take the laces out. That's right, now cut them in two. Don't pull anything from your pocket but a knife. Right."

He stepped a little to one side. "Now pitch the knife into the other room, under the bed," he ordered. He gestured again to Hatfield. "Now lie down on your face, on the floor, and put your hands behind your back, together," he directed.

Seething with helpless rage, the Lone Wolf obeyed.

"Take two of those thongs and tie his hands and ankles," the gunman told Welch. "Do a good job. I'll look at the knots after you're finished, and if they're not right—well, you'll never tie another. Drop the other two thongs on the floor."

Welch did as he was told, and was ordered to lie down beside Hatfield. Their captor crossed the room, circling the prostrate forms, holstered one gun and with his free hand swiftly noosed Welch's wrists and ankles. Then he crossed to the lamp and blew it out. With unhesitating steps he walked to the door.

"Guess you'll stay put now," was his parting shot as he banged the door shut after him.

Silence fell in the room, broken only by Welch's gurgled profanity.

But when, a little later, the gunman's steps had died away, Welch instantly ceased swearing.

"Hatfield," he said in a hoarse whisper. "I didn't shut the blade of my knife when I pitched it into the other room. It's under the bunk. If you can roll in there and get it, mebbe we can cut each other loose."

"Quick thinking, feller!" applauded the Ranger. "I'll make a try at it, anyhow."

Squirming and jerking, he slowly rolled his body across the floor. Negotiating the door was difficult, but he finally made it and, after several efforts, managed to writhe under the low bunk. The only way he could look for the knife was with his face and his body, and the blade proved to be elusive. He was still squirming and writhing about when Welch called hoarsely from the outer room:

"Feller, do yuh smell somethin' burnin'?"

Hatfield sniffed sharply. The acrid tang of wood smoke stung his nostrils.

"The horned toad has set the house afire!" Welch squawked from the other room. "Hustle, feller, or we'll be roasted like pigs in a barbecue!"

Hatfield renewed his efforts to find the knife. After an eternity of frantic and futile groping, his bound wrists felt the touch of solid steel. He managed to jerk his body down toward the foot of the bunk, doubling himself up as he did so. Snuffling and nosing the floor with his face, he finally made contact and managed to grip the handle of the knife between his teeth.

The return trip across the room was agonizingly difficult, hampered as he was with the knife in his jaw. He was soaked with perspiration and trembling in every muscle when he at length barged into Welch's prostrate form. The room was thick with smoke and an ominous crackling sounded. The window square was already glowing dully as the flames got firm hold on the tinder-dry boards of the shanty.

With a prodigy of effort, Hatfield managed to set the blade of the knife against the thong that bound the watchman's wrists. He began to saw the blade up and down, exerting all the pressure that was possible. His neck was a fiery ache and his jaw muscles throbbed and burned. The smoke was growing thicker and Hatfield was forced to madly resist an almost uncontrollable desire to cough. If he did so, the knife would fly from his mouth and he would be forced to grope and hunt for it again.

Welch winced as the sharp steel rasped against his flesh.

"Don't mind cuttin' me," he gasped. "I can take it. Hustle, feller, the fire's comin' through the wall!"

The room was no longer dark. An angry glow revealed objects. A tongue of flame writhed through the wall boards, drew back like a startled snake, flickered through once more, stronger and more persistent. The air was stifling hot, sapping the Ranger's strength, numbing his brain.

"Oh, why did I hafta go and put new strings in them damn boots!" moaned Welch as the stubborn cords resisted the sawing steel.

Hatfield felt his strength going. He trembled so he could hardly hold the knife between his teeth. His movements were jerky and lacked coordination. He heard Welch gasp as the blade bit deep into his wrist. Then suddenly the cord parted. Welch jerked and twisted, the loosened bonds fell away and his hands were free. He writhed over on his face, groped upward and gripped the knife handle. Hatfield flopped onto his face and with a few swift strokes Welch severed the thong that bound the Ranger's wrists. Then he freed Hatfield's ankles and his own. They staggered to their numbed feet.

"Not a minute too soon, either," the watchman gasped. "That wall's ready to fall in!"

Hatfield lurched to the corner of the room where his guns lay. He fumbled them up, managed to buckle the belts about his waist.

"Come on," he panted to Welch, and reeled to the door. He jerked the knob, threw his weight forcibly against it; but the door stood firm and did not move.

"My God, there's a padlock on the outside. That skunk has locked us in!" wailed Welch.

Hatfield hurled his great weight at the door. It creaked and groaned, but solidly resisted his efforts. He glanced wildly around the room.

"The table!" he panted. "Grab holt, feller!"

Together they hurled the clumsy battering ram against the door. A board splintered. They tried again, but still the door would not open. The room was like an oven, filled with fire and smoke. The weakened wall was creaking and groaning.

"Once more!" panted the Ranger. "Everything yuh've got!"

With the last strength of desperation they flung the battered table at the door, their combined weights behind it.

The planks splintered, burst outward. One more blow and there was an opening big enough to squeeze through. Hatfield shoved Welch into it and, the instant he had cleared, writhed after him. Just as he reached the outer air, the wall fell in with a thundering crash and the whole shanty was a welter of flame.

They reeled away from the burning building, breathing the cool night air in great gulps. The scene was as light as day as the flames roared upward.

A single glance showed no waiting horses. There was a light in the office of the mill, but nobody was in sight.

Taking a chance, guns out and ready, Hatfield raced to the open door.

The office was silent and deserted. The vault door stood wide. No silver bricks littered the floor. He bounded inside. One look was enough. The vault had been rifled of its contents.

Quietly Jim Hatfield holstered his guns. He fished the makin's from his pocket and rolled a cigarette.

"Well, they put it over, and put it over good!" he remarked to Welch.

"They shore did," agreed that worthy. "Feller, I've a plumb workin' hunch that big jigger musta been Jose Muerta. Ain't nobody else hereabouts in the owlhoot game got that much savvy. Not that I've ever heard tell of. Uh-huh, it musta been Muerta."

Hatfield said nothing, but his eyes were coldly gray as water torturing under ice.

"What I can't understand," wondered Welch, "is why that skunk didn't shoot us down when we stepped inter the shanty."

"That's where he showed himself plumb smart once again," Hatfield replied. "Men sometimes take a heap of killin', and even after they're shot fatal have been knowed to get a gun out and kill the jigger what downs them. He figgered that, and acted according. He knew plumb well we wouldn't make a move when he had the dead drop on us that way. Where he slipped was in not plugging us both after we were tied up. He showed a weak streak there. Mean as a hyderphobia skunk and wanted to make us cash in in as unpleasant a way as possible. Wanted to think of us being roasted alive in that burning shanty. Uh-huh, that's where he slipped, and slipped bad."

Tom Welch, glancing at the Lone Wolf's bleak face and terrible eyes, was inclined to agree.

Suddenly remembering something, Hatfield strode to the door and glanced out. The body of the slain owlhoot had vanished.

"Took him along with them; scairt somebody would recognize him, chances are," he deduced. "Uh-huh, a plumb cultus outfit with plenty of savvy. They didn't ride far when they hightailed away from here the fust time. That jigger snuk back over the hill and holed up in the shanty, figgering we'd come there sooner or later. Then after he hawgtied us, he signaled to his men to come on—mebbe setting fire to the shanty was the signal. Then they cleaned out the vault and left. Uh-huh, plenty of savvy."

Morning was breaking in rose and gold in the east. Welch glanced at his watch.

"Past six," he announced. "Somebody had oughta be here within a hour at most."

They were there in considerably less than an hour. Men returning to the mine saw the glare of the burning shanty and pushed their horses. There was a babble of questions, much profanity.

"Come on, Hatfield," Welch said at length, "time we were headin' for town and the sheriff's office. I got a horse in that shed where yuh put yores. Lucky it was far enough away from the shanty not to ketch fire too."

Together they rode for town. They passed wagonloads of miners coming back to work, others on horseback or in buckboards, but they did not pause, answering the greetings shouted to them with waves of their hands.

On arriving at the sheriff's office, they found a fat, jolly little man with twinkling eyes seated at the sheriff's desk.

"Craig headed out of town an hour back," he replied to their question. "Headed for the Slash K spread way down in the southwest tip of the county. Jose Muerta widelooped a big herd down there a mite before midnight last night."

TEN

Jim Hatfield stared at the fat little deputy. "How yuh know it was Muerta did the widelooping?" he asked.

"Cowhand feller they failed to cash in got a good look at the hellion," the deputy replied cheerfully. "It was him brought the word here, rode all night. From his description of the hellion leadin' the outfit, it couldn't have been anybody but Muerta. *Don* Jose is purty well known hereabouts and the description fitted him to a T."

"Then it wasn't Muerta up to the mine after all!" exploded Welch. "It's nigh onto fifty miles to the Slash K."

"Couldn't very well have been in both places at once," Hatfield replied noncommittally, the concentration furrow deep between his black brows.

"Eh! What's that?" exclaimed the deputy. "What's that about the mine?"

Hatfield told him, in terse sentences. The deputy became all activity.

"Come on over to the bank!" he exclaimed. "John Mosby is there. Gotta tell him about it."

Mosby listened to the story of the robbery in grim silence. He fixed his hard little eyes on Hatfield's face, turned his gaze to Welch.

"Tom," he squeaked, "if I hadn't knowed yuh for close onto forty years, and yore father before yuh, I'd be sorta inclined to say it was a inside job and that you and this cowboy wasn't tellin' all yuh know!"

Welch bristled, but Hatfield merely nodded and remarked in quiet tones:

"Can't say as I'd blame yuh."

"Not that I'm accusin' either of yuh," Mosby hastened to add. "I know Welch too well to believe any such thing of him, and you, feller, don't look pertickler like the owlhoot kind. Go over it again, and let me be shore I get the straight of everything."

Hatfield and Welch repeated the story, adding detail. Mosby tugged at his mustache, wagged his head and squeaked cuss words.

"Shore sounds like some of Muerta's work," he declared, "but it couldn't have been, not with him rustlin' cattle from the Slash K only a few hours before it happened. The hellion ain't got wings, I reckon. Hell's fire and blazes! are we up against two outfits of that sort? There won't nothin' be safe from now on!"

He glanced at the wall clock. "After ten," he said. "I sorta feel the need of a drink."

He turned to his cashier, who had joined them in the office. "I'm droppin' over to the Anytime," he announced. "When Mr. Dawson comes in, tell him—"

Just then the tapping of a cane sounded and Lynn Dawson entered the office. He was introduced to Hatfield, with whom he shook hands with a firm grip, peering with squinted eyes through his colored lenses, his face less than a foot from the Ranger's.

The story was repeated for Dawson's benefit.

"Mr. Mosby, don't yuh figger we'd oughta send for the Rangers?" the cashier tentatively suggested.

Old John snorted like a bull in a cactus patch.

"Rangers!" he squealed wrathfully. "What damn good are the Rangers! Texas would be better off without them. Time was when they were all right, but they've gone to seed—skatin' along on their rep'tation. Muerta and his gang has been makin' monkeys out of 'em! Uh-huh, we'd be better off without 'em, and after next election, chances are we'll get rid of 'em. They done outlived their usefulness."

"I can't agree with you there, John," said Lynn Dawson in his quiet voice. "The Rangers are the greatest force for law and order in Texas, and the most feared by outlaws."

Mosby sputtered and squeaked. "I'll take Craig Wilson against all the blankety-blanked Rangers," he declared. "If anybody runs Muerta down, it'll be Craig. Now that the hellion has started op'ratin' in Craig's county, you see if he don't! Come on, you fellers, let's go get that drink. Hatfield, we'll want you to stick around until the sheriff gets back. He'll want to have a gab with yuh."

"Yeah, I'll stick," Hatfield replied, with a meaning that was not conveyed to his hearers.

After a drink or two in the Anytime, Hatfield accompanied Welch to the doctor's office to have his cut head dressed and plastered up.

"Nothin' to worry about," was the old frontier doctor's verdict. "Yuh've had wuss from scratchin' yoreself."

Leaving the doctor's office, Hatfield hunted up a livery stable for his horse. He obtained a room for himself on the second floor of the stable, over the stalls and alongside the haymow. Welch, meanwhile, had returned to the Anytime, where Hatfield joined him a little later. He found the watchman at the end of the bar, engaged in conversation with John Mosby. The old cattleman greeted Hatfield cordially, and ordered him a drink.

"Been havin' a little gab with Tom," he announced. "After thinkin' things over, Hatfield, I figger yuh did a good chore up at the mine, though that hellion did put one over on yuh. Anyhow, yuh made the skunks work for what they got, and I've a notion yuh hit 'em hard by downin' that one yuh cashed in. Jiggers what can work the combination of a safe ain't easy to come by, and they'll miss that sidewinder. Pity

116

yuh didn't down the big skookum he-wolf of the pack at the same time. That's where the brains of the outfit is or I'm a heap mistook. I figger that jigger really was Muerta, after all. Chances are it was some other pack of coyotes what widelooped that herd down to the Slash K. That cowboy got a glim of a tall feller with light-colored hair and nacherly jumped to the conclusion it was Muerta, him havin' raised so much hell in this end of Texas of late. Reckon everybody what has somethin' off color happen to 'em are seein' Muerta fust off. So far as I can judge, that was a ord'nary run-of-mine wideloopin', the kind any stray bunch of owlhoots pull off. The mine job had the true Muerta brand."

"The feller what hawgtied us shore had yaller hair, all right," put in Welch, "and he was big and tall and talked soft and easy, like they say Muerta talks. Ain't that right, Hatfield?"

Hatfield nodded, but refrained from comment. Old John tugged his mustache.

"After yuh see the sheriff when he gets back, I'd like to have a little gab with yuh, Hatfield," he announced. "You just passin' through, or was yuh figgerin' on stickin' around for a spell?"

"Looks like a sorta nice section," the Ranger replied.

"It is," Mosby agreed emphatically, "or was till hell started bustin' loose, but I don't reckon that'll last. Craig Wilson will drop a loop on them hellions quicker'n a steer can switch his tail in fly time. Yeah, it's a good country. We'll have a gab together."

He let the matter rest there, and headed back to the bank to take care of unfinished business.

"John is all right," said Welch. "He's sorta put out over what happened last night, but yuh can't blame him. That was a hefty passel of dinero them skunks packed off, and John owns the controllin' interest in the Silver City. Not that he's over hurt by the loss—he's got plenty—but he allus hated for somebody to put somethin' over on him. I figger he's sorta took a shine to yuh, Hatfield. Yuh'd do well to get in with him. He does good by his hands."

Hatfield nodded, but again refrained from comment.

"Let's drop down the street to the Greasy Sack," Welch suggested. "It's the biggest place in town. Pecos Rose runs it, and she's some gal."

Hatfield agreed, and they left the Anytime.

Pecos Rose had masses of flaming red hair that was really beautiful. Her figure left little to be desired. Her nose reminded Hatfield of a sunburned cucumber, and she had a jaw like a hammerhead roan's. But there were humorous lines at the corners of her soft brown eyes and she had a quick smile that rendered her face, which was rather grim in repose, very pleasant.

Hatfield was of the opinion that, despite her nose and her jaw, he could very easily learn to like this lady saloonkeeper.

Pecos Rose greeted them with a nod and a wave of a slim hand blazing with diamonds, and then, apparently, forgot all about them.

"But she sees everything what goes on," Welch confided to Hatfield. "She's givin' yuh a thorough goin' over in the back bar mirror right now."

Which was a fact that Hatfield had already noted.

"She's that way with strangers," Welch added, "and she don't often make mistakes. Funny, the folks she ain't got no use for—some of 'em folks most ev'body else thinks well of. Tell yuh more about that later. And, inc'dentally, I'll back Rose's judgment of a feller agin anybody else's, even if I can't see inter it."

Despite the fact that it was little past mid-afternoon, the bar and tables of the Greasy Sack were well patronized. It was a boisterous crowd, but Hatfield felt that it was gayer and more carefree than that which he had seen at the Anytime.

"But it's full of dynamite," he mused, "with all those hell-raisin' young punchers getting hot under their belts. Most anything is liable to happen here."

However, the bartenders and floor men had an

efficient look and were doubtless able to cope with any situation that might arise.

"Games here are plumb square," Welch remarked. "Rose sees to that. Usually straight enough at the Anytime, too, but after all, the Anytime is just a sort of plaything for John Mosby. John has heaps of other interests and can't keep a eye on things like Rose does here. You know how it is—a crooked dealer will slip in every now and then, if yuh don't watch 'em almighty close. John throwed one through a window last week. Feller was caught cold-deckin'. But it came mighty nigh to a bad shootin'."

They spent some time in the Greasy Sack, enjoyed a prime helpin' of chuck, and then gave the town the once-over.

"Salty," was Hatfield's verdict, "plenty salty, and liable to be interestin'. I've a notion I didn't play a wrong hunch when I came here. What happened last night sorta proves it."

They returned to the Anytime just as dusk was falling, and found John Mosby in a very bad temper.

"Wilson would go gallivantin' off somewhere at a time like this," he complained. "Didn't leave nobody in the office but fat Bill Brady, his clerk. If he'd been here, or even Skeeter Ellis, his chief deputy, they mighta got a posse together and trailed them hellions to their hole-up. But now they got such a start nobody will ever ketch 'em up."

But Mosby's peeve was mild compared to that of Sheriff Craig Wilson when, something after midnight, he entered the saloon, powdered with dust and bearing other marks of long and hard riding.

"John," he barked without preamble, "did you happen to recognize that dawn cowpuncher what brought us word of the wideloopin' as a Slash K hand?"

"Never seed him before, so far as I rec'lect," Mosby disclaimed. "All I noticed about him was that he was a dark, almost Mexican lookin' feller and rode a horse with a Slash K brand. Why?"

"*He'll* wear a slash brand, and it won't be a K, if I ever lay eyes on him again!" Wilson promised viciously. "That hellion rode back with us, yuh'll rec'lect. About a couple of miles from the Slash K his hoss went lame, which didn't 'pear surprisin', seein' as he'd made a fast round trip without hardly any rest. Well, this feller lagged behind and the rest of us rode on fast. That's the last we seed of the sidewinder. When we got to the Slash K, old Caleb Clingman give us blue blazin' hell for wakin' him up from his afternoon nap. He said he hadn't heard anythin' about any wideloopin' on his place and if there had been he reckoned he'd have knowed of it. Said he never sent nobody to town for the sheriff and wanted to know if the hull kit and kaboodle of us was plumb loco. So we sifted sand back to town, tol'ble fast. Now what the hell's this all about?"

"I figger I can tell yuh," Mosby squeaked grimly. He regaled the sheriff with an account of the happenings at the Silver City mine the night before.

Salty Craig Wilson swore until there was a purple halo around his head and the air sniffed of brimstone. He glowered accusingly at Welch and Hatfield, and centered his interest on the Ranger.

"Reckon yuh're okay, from what Welch says," he growled, "but yuh got a gun slingin' look about yuh. I'm tellin' yuh right now, while yuh're in this section, keep them hawglegs of yores penned!"

The Lone Wolf's lips quirked slightly at the corners. "Sorry," he drawled ironically, "sorry I didn't meet up with yuh yesterday. Never 'curred to me yuh might object when I pulled 'em last night. Plumb sorry, Sheriff."

Wilson flushed angrily. "Don't go gettin' funny!" he barked. "Yuh know damn well what I mean. Yuh didn't do so much, lettin' them hellions put one over thataway."

"Reckon mebbe yuh're right there," Hatfield agreed unexpectedly. "Been thinking sorta the same thing myself."

"Well, if yuh have yuh got more sense than most have," Sheriff Wilson returned. "That's to yore credit, anyhow. So long, John, I'm gonna get somethin' to eat."

He hitched his cartridge belt higher and stumped off. Mosby watched him go with a chuckle.

"Craig's bark is wuss than his bite, where decent fellers is concerned," he told Hatfield. "Reckon he's feelin' sorta put out about now. It was nice of yuh, Hatfield, not to remind him of how he had one put over on *him*."

"I'll let him think of it himself, later," Hatfield smiled.

Mosby moved away and, a little later, Hatfield saw him laughing and joking with one of his floor men.

"Doesn't take his loss of last night over hard," Hatfield remarked to Welch.

The watchman shrugged his shoulders. "Oh, John hasn't anythin' to worry about," he replied. "He told me a little while ago that the shipment was insured for full value. John don't stand to lose anythin'."

Hatfield stared at his informant, but said nothing.

Later that night, in his little room over the stalls, Hatfield reviewed the situation in his mind while he carefully cleaned and oiled his guns.

"Uh-huh, a plumb smart outfit," he mused. "Soon as they left the mine last night, they sent a feller hightailin' to town to hand the sheriff that blotted-brand yarn about the widelooping down at the Slash K. Figgered it would get him outa the way before the word got to town of the robbery. They couldn't move fast with those heavy bricks, and a feller plumb familiar with the section, like the sheriff would be, might be able to figger out where they would head for. Uh-huh, they think of everything. This is getting more interesting all the time."

He slipped fresh cartridges into the cylinders of the Colts and holstered one. He addressed the other confidentially, in the fashion of men who ride much alone and form the habit of talking to their horses, or even to their guns.

"And so Mosby doesn't stand to lose anything by that robbery, eh? And Welch told me it was the fust time he ever had a cleanup insured. Looks almost like he was expecting something to happen to this one. Well, he played his hunch right, if it was a hunch. Funny thing is how did that hellion, Muerta, if it was him, know the cleanup was still at the mine. From all I could learn, it was supposed to come to Alamita two days before. That's what everybody seemed to believe. And the Silver City folks even played it up so strong they didn't even post a special guard at the mine last night, with all the hands in town celebrating. Looks like they sorta overplayed their hand there. Was the logical thing to do, though, with the cleanup supposed to be already in town. Didn't fool the gents who lifted it, though. Yes, it's looking more and more like Muerta's work, all right. He has the rep'tation of being able to learn about things he's not supposed to know. Has connections, all right, and I'm figgering they're right here in Alamita. Well, it's my chore to find out fust off who those connections are. Do that, and getting a line on Muerta ought to be easy."

Placing his guns where they were within hands' reach, he went to bed.

Hatfield slept soundly, but in Alamita there were those who did not sleep. In a closely shuttered room, dimly lighted by a single lamp, a group of men sat around a table and conversed earnestly in low tones. Sheriff Wilson would have been enraged and scandalized if he had known that one of the men in the room was Jose Muerta, lounging gracefully at one end of the table, a cigarette between his slim fingers. Around him were grouped several of his dark-skinned Yaqui fighters.

There were other men in the room, men who were not Yaquis and who had not first seen the light south of the Rio Grande. They were hard of face, tight of mouth, with keen, watchful eyes and with hands that never seemed to stray far from the weapons hanging at their belts. They said little, and what they did say was terse and to the point.

At the far end of the table, where the shadows were deepest, his hatbrim drawn low over his eyes, sat a man to whom even the swaggering Muerta listened with respectful attention.

"Something's got to be done about that seven-foot hellion," he was saying. "Something's got to be done before he makes us real trouble. I'm mighty suspicion of his showing up just at this time. How did he happen to be up there at the mine last night? It looks mighty funny. He's bad, and he's smart. Getting out of that burning shanty as he did proves that. The job last night was handled pretty well, but not well enough. It cost us a good man. Crowley will be hard to replace, and until he is replaced, I'll have to do his work myself, and there are plenty of reasons why I shouldn't have to do it. If the job had been pulled as we planned, it would have puzzled everybody. As it was, it was altogether too spectacular and has set people to talking and guessing. Which is just what we didn't want to have happen. If it had been pulled as we planned, nobody would have been seen and suspicion might have fallen upon somebody concerned with the mine up there. As it is, everybody feels it is an outside job and are acting accordingly, and all because of what appears to be a wandering cowboy."

"But who and what in blazes is he if he isn't a cowboy?" asked one of the hard-faced Texans.

"That remains to be found out," replied the man at the end of the table. "A Cattleman's Association rider, perhaps, or an insurance company investigator. Remember that Sanders bank was insured, as was that gold shipment over to the west. Anyhow, he'll bear watching, and more than watching."

"I'd like to meet him alone on the trail!" Muerta blustered. "I'd—"

"*Die!*" the other cut in. "I'm willing to wager any amount that he can beat your draw without exerting himself. I'm not at all sure that I can shade him myself, with everything even, and I can make you look like a snail climbing a slick log. That's not the way to handle this thing, Muerta. You're always talking about your brains—well, use them!"

"I will," hissed Muerta, speaking perfect English with scant trace of accent, his musical voice deadly with menace.

"It's your chore," said the man at the end of the table.

Muerta turned to one of his swarthy retainers.

"You kept a line on him all evening, Felipe?" he asked.

"*Si, Capitan,*" replied the *teniente.* "All his moves I know, and where he is to be found."

"*Bueno!*" exclaimed Muerta. He spoke for a moment in rapid Spanish.

"You understand?" he asked at length.

"*Si,* perfectly, *Capitan,*" returned Felipe, his beady eyes glittering with an evil light. "*Si,* I will not fail. It will be most simple."

The man who had spoken a moment before moved restlessly in his chair.

"I don't like this hull business," he complained. "We're raisin' too much hell. Ord'nary killin's don't attract over much attention, but plain snuk-in-the-dark murder does. Fust thing we know we'll be havin' Rangers over here."

"Rangers! Who cares for the Rangers—" Muerta began contemptuously. The man at the far end of the table cut him short.

"Don't go underestimating the Rangers," he said. "We certainly don't want them here—yet. So far, thanks chiefly to John Mosby's political connections, we've been able to keep them away. The Rangers are what we have to look out for more than anything else. Later perhaps it will be a different story, but not now. It's because of the Rangers that I decided to start operating over in this section. Craig Wilson is stubborn as a blue-nosed mule and he has a mighty fine opinion of his ability as a sheriff. He won't ask for Ranger help—he'll fight against it, and Mosby will back him up. Before Wilson realizes he has more than he can handle, it'll be too late. But that fellow Hatfield must be taken care of. Our plans are building up nicely and it's almost time for the first big move. I don't propose to have everything spoiled by a damn range tramp. On your way, Felipe!"

Grinning evilly, the Yaqui lieutenant slid snakily from the room on his mission of murder.

ELEVEN

Jim Hatfield was aroused, or rather shot from his slumbers by an awful cry of agony and terror. His hair bristled and the palms of his hands grew clammily moist as that terrible cry rang in his ears.

Mingled with the anguished shriek was a thrashing and thudding, and the horrible scream of a maddened horse.

For seconds the frightful duet continued, then it shut off as suddenly as it began. There remained but a sickening sound as of a great dog worrying something to death.

Hatfield leaped from the bed, seizing his guns. He heard a thud of feet on the floor of the room next to his, and the voice of the old stablekeeper roaring profanity. He rushed to the door, gripped the knob. Then he abruptly realized that he would be silhouetted against the open window across the room. He swung to one side, hugging the wall, and with a quick jerk flung the door wide open.

There was a thundering crash. Flame seemed to gush clear across the room. Buckshot hissed through the open door and tore the window to tinkling fragments.

Instinctively Hatfield fired three quick shots

through the door. He heard the bullets thud against the wall. Silence followed, save for the crunching and thrashing about and the snorting of the enraged horse in the stall below.

Another door banged open. The stablekeeper appeared, bare of feet, clad in a long nightshirt, a lamp in one hand and a cocked Sharps buffalo rifle in the other.

"What the hell's going on here?" he bellowed.

Hatfield was staring at what the light of the lamp revealed.

Roped to the newel post of the stair, which was directly opposite the door of his room, was a sawed-off shotgun with its twin muzzles trained to sweep the door. A broken cord trailed from the triggers. The cord had been passed around the post and its far end tied to the door knob.

"So that anybody opening the door and stepping through would get both barrels dead center," the Ranger muttered to himself. He experienced a crawling of his flesh as he recalled how he had barely checked himself before flinging open the door and rushing into the hall.

"But what the blankety-blank—" began the bewildered stablekeeper.

Hatfield checked him with a gesture.

"Hold it, Hank," he said quietly. "Bring the lamp and come on downstairs. Steady, now, though I don't reckon there's anything else to worry about, judging from those yells we heard.

I figger I know what happened down there."

His face was bleak as he cautiously led the way downstairs, his guns ready. Old Hank, the stable-keeper, followed close behind him, the lamp held high. He clucked under his breath as the rays fell on a wrathful golden head looming from the nearest stall. Goldy's ears were laid back, his eyes rolled and his nostrils flared redly. His lips were writhed back to reveal gleaming white teeth, and those teeth were blotched and streaked with awful stains.

Hatfield's breath caught sharply as he realized the nature of those stains, although he had expected something of the sort. Old Hank swore weakly as he peered at the torn and mangled thing that lay beneath the sorrel's iron hoofs.

"Come out, Goldy," Hatfield quietly ordered.

The sorrel came out of the stall, stepping gingerly over the broken, bloody mass of flesh that had once been a man. Hatfield passed a soothing hand along his sleek neck and the sorrel stopped shivering and snorting and stood regarding him with great liquid eyes.

Old Hank held the lamp into the stall. "Did the hellion try to lift the hoss out of the stable?" he demanded.

Something lying on the floor caught the lamp-light in a twinkling gleam. Hatfield picked it up. It was a long and heavy-bladed knife with a horn handle. He held it to the light.

"Was he tryin' to kill the critter, or hamstring him?" Hank exclaimed.

"Don't figger it that way," Hatfield replied quietly, running a finger along the keen edge. "I figger he just aimed to devil the horse with the point and start him raisin' hell. Then, of co'hse, he figgered, we'd come runnin' out upstairs to see what was wrong; and that sawed-off up there would get in its licks. He made a bad mistake. Reckon he started to use the knife on Goldy, and Goldy, who's never tied in his stall, got him."

"I'll say he did!" muttered Hank, peering at the horribly torn and trampled corpse, and shuddering. "Feller, that was one awful way to die—nothin' wuss than bein' bit and stomped by a mad hoss! No wonder he yelled!

"But the sneakin' hyderphobia skunk had it comin'!" he stormed, abruptly realizing to the full the meaning of the shotgun clamped to the newel post. "Tryin' to drygulch a man thataway. Good hoss!"

Fearlessly he stroked the reeking muzzle. The sorrel whinnied softly and thrust his velvety muzzle into the gnarled old hand.

"Goldy doesn't make any mistakes where folks are concerned," Hatfield said. "But he's not a horse to fool with."

"I'll say he ain't," Hank agreed emphatically. "But, son, what's this all about? Why did—"

He ceased speaking abruptly as the stable

door swung open and a man stood revealed in the lamplight. It was Skeeter Ellis, the lanky, humorous deputy sheriff. But there was no laughter in his eyes at the moment and his mouth was a hard line. One sinewy hand rested on the butt of his gun.

"That's what I wanta know, what's this all about," he repeated Hank's words. "Who shot out the window upstairs, and what was that awful yellin'? We heard it clean over on Chuckwalla Street. What's goin' on here?"

In a few brief sentences Hatfield informed him of what had happened. Old Hank nodded corroboration to the Ranger's statements.

Ellis peered at the dead man and made a wry face. "Ain't over purty, is he?" he commented. "Hold the lamp, Hank, and let's see if we can find out what he looked like when he was alive."

The dead man had a swarthy, vicious face dominated by a hawklike beak of a nose. His cheekbones were high, his hair was lank and black, cut in a bang across his low forehead. On his vicious countenance was stamped a look of terror and agony that even the hand of death had not been able to smooth away.

"Pure blood Yaqui, or I'm a heap mistook," was Ellis' diagnosis. Hatfield nodded agreement.

The deputy stared at him speculatively. "Looks like, feller," he remarked at length, "that yuh've made yoreself some purty bad enemies. Uh-huh,

I reckon it was Muerta the other night, all right. This looks like some of his work—he never forgets or forgives a bad turn—and this hellion has all the earmarks of bein' one of his Yaquis. Feller, my advice to you is to hit the trail outa this section pronto, and ride fast."

"Thanks," Hatfield replied quietly. "I'm not taking it."

"Didn't figger yuh would," admitted Ellis. "Well, let's haul this sidewinder outa the stall and lay him over to one side till the sheriff and the coroner sees him, so the hoss can get some sleep."

"Reckon that's good advice for the rest of us," Hatfield said, after they had disposed of the body. "My room is nice and airy now."

"Mebbe you'll get some more ear poundin' tonight, but I won't," growled old Hank. "I'll be layin' with one eye open and this buffaler gun leanin' against the bed. Somebody might come lookin' for that sidewinder."

"Not much chance, I reckon," Hatfield replied. "Guess this hull end of town is purty well roused up."

"It is," grunted Ellis. "We'd have had a crowd in here by now, only I ordered 'em to keep away. Reckon the sheriff will want to have another gab with yuh come t'morrow, Hatfield."

Sheriff Wilson did. He glared at Hatfield when the latter reported at his office the following morning, per Ellis' suggestion.

"Why in blazes did yuh hafta coil yore twine in this section?" he wailed indignantly. "The minute you landed things began happenin'. Was plumb peaceful till you showed up."

"Mebbe it'll be peaceful again after I leave," Hatfield remarked with a significance that was lost on the sheriff.

"I don't doubt it a mite," Sheriff Wilson agreed heartily. "Why don't yuh go away?"

"Sorta like the section," Hatfield replied amiably. "Seems sorta nice and sociable, the way gents drop in on yuh any hour of the day or night. Reckon I'll stick around a spell and see if I can't meet some more nice folks."

Sheriff Wilson snorted his disgust. "By the way," he grumbled, "John Mosby wants yuh to drop in at the bank and see him. Asked me to tell yuh. No, there's nothin' more I wanta talk to yuh about. We'll hold an inquest on that hellion this afternoon. You and Hank be there to testify. Needn't bring the hoss. He did his chore last night and, everythin' considered, I gotta admit it was a plumb good one. Wouldn't mind over much if yuh left the hoss when yuh decide to pull out."

"Scairt old Goldy would be sorta lonesome without me," Hatfield smiled as he left the office and headed for the bank.

He found old John Mosby at his desk. Mosby nodded pleasantly and offered him a chair. For some moments he sat drumming on his desk and giving the Lone Wolf a careful once-over with his little, deep-set eyes.

"Son, I gathered from what yuh said yesterday yuh wouldn't mind stickin' around this section for a spell?" he remarked interrogatively.

"Reckon that's right," Hatfield agreed.

"Well," continued Mosby, "that'd sorta suit me, pertickler if you and me can get together."

"Meaning?"

"Meanin' that I've sorta took a shine to yuh, son, and I figger I could use yuh. That robbery the other night sorta shook me up a mite. The cleanup they got was insured. I sorta played a hunch and had that cleanup insured. Did it on my own. Didn't tell anybody I was goin' to do it, not even Lynn Dawson, my manager. Folks hereabouts kinda figger a thing like that for damphoolishness and a waste of money. Usta figger that way myself. Mighty glad I changed my mind all of a sudden. That was the fust cleanup I ever insured, and from what I heerd this mornin', it's liable to be the last. I hadda pay plenty to insure them bricks, but it was a mighty good investment. The insurance representative was here to see me this mornin', and he was fit to be tied. He quoted rates I'd hafta pay on any other cleanup I might want to insure, and them rates are plumb ruinous. Can't afford to pay 'em, and after what happened the other night,

I can't afford to take any chances with future cleanups."

He paused to stuff tobacco into his pipe and get it alight. Hatfield took advantage of the opportunity to roll a cigarette.

When his pipe was going good, Mosby began speaking again.

"Most everything I've got is invested in the Silver City," he announced. "My spread and my place across the street, and my bank stock are all tied up in it. A good investment, all right, if things go smoothly. I've decided to stamp my ore here in town in the near future. I need a new stamp mill. The one up to the mine isn't near big enough to properly take care of the output. I'm going to build another one here in town. And I'm goin' to install an overhead conveyor system to bring the ore down from the mine."

"It beats hauling," Hatfield agreed. "It's a long pull and yuh'll need relay engines along the route, but it'll pay in the end, if the mine is a big producer."

Mosby regarded him curiously. "Yuh seem to know somethin' about it, son," he remarked. He continued without waiting for Hatfield to comment.

"Yes, I'm gonna install conveyors, and increase the output. The lode up there is rich and deep. I figger it ain't so over far from equalin' what the Comstock usta be up Nevada way. There's one

137

awful heap of dinero to be made from the Silver City, and I figger to make it."

Hatfield regarded him, a curious look in his green eyes.

"What yuh want such a heap of money for, Mosby, at yore age?" he asked suddenly.

Old John smiled slightly. "Yuh'd never guess," he replied. "Well, yuh don't need to; I'll tell yuh. Hatfield, it's like this. I've had a good life, made plenty of money, lived well, enjoyed myself. Texas and this section of Texas in pertickler give it to me. Now that I'm gettin' on, I feel that I'd oughta sorta do somethin' to pay it back. I ain't got nobody—nobody—dependin' on me."

A shadow flitted across his fat face as he made the statement, and he pulled hard on his pipe. An instant later, however, he shrugged his big shoulders as if shaking off some invisible load.

"No, I ain't got nobody," he repeated. "But I figger I got responsibilities. Hatfield, there's folks comin' inter this section, which I figger will some day be one of the best in all Texas. Up nawth of my spread, the Bar M, folks are comin' in and settlin'. Pore folks, mostly, who take up a little patch of land and work hard to make a livin' off it. Little alfalfa farmers, and fellers with a few head of cattle, and the like. Them fellers and their kids deserve somethin' better'n what they are gettin'. They're makin' a livin', but that's about all. Their kids won't have the advantages that—that some folks' kids have had. I figger they'd oughta have them. I figger they need good schools—need a big university near by the kids can go to and get proper eddicatin'. I never had much myself, and there's been times when I missed it mighty bad. But things like that cost money, heaps of money. I aims to make a heap of money, and use it that way—to build a nice town in this section, not a hell raiser like this Alamita, but a real nice town with schools and mebbe a church or two, and a university. That's what I aims to do, Hatfield, with the money I figger to make outa the Silver City. As I said, I've sunk about everythin' I own in that mine, and everythin' depends on its goin' along smooth, producin' like it can, and gettin' what it produces to the proper market. If I'd lost all that cleanup represented the other night, it woulda give me a bad jolt and set me back. I ain't gonna take any more chances. And that brings me down to you."

Hatfield regarded the fat, gross looking man, a warm light in his strangely colored eyes.

"Reckon the Lord don't pay over much attention to the outside coverin' when he sets out to make a *man,*" he mused to himself. "It's what goes inside the package that counts."

Aloud he said, "I'll be glad to help yuh, suh, if I can."

"Yuh can," Mosby declared with emphasis. "I got yuh branded as a purty salty hombre, Hatfield, and, what's better, a feller with somethin' under his hat besides hair. What I propose to do is hire a force of guards to look after my property to see that things like what happened the other night don't happen again. Somethin' is buildin' up in this section, unless I'm a heap mistook, somethin' what will mean big trouble for decent folks, if it ain't put down before it gets a good start. Yeah, I'm gonna hire guards and put them on the job, and I want yuh to take charge of 'em. Yuh'll have all the authority yuh need, and I'll back yuh up to the tie end of yore rope. What do yuh say?"

Hatfield stood up. He smiled down at the old man from his great height, his green eyes sunny as summer seas, his stern face all of a sudden wonderfully pleasant.

"I reckon, suh," he said in his deep, musical voice, "yuh done hired yoreself a hand."

With Mosby's approval, Hatfield proceeded to get together his force of guards. The nucleus of the outfit was formed of several of Mosby's Bar M cowhands, rollicking young punchers who were ready for anything from a frolic to a fight and were not particular as to which it should be, just so plenty of excitement was promised. Several hands from neighboring spreads, attracted by the high wages offered, volunteered their services.

Hatfield chose his men with care, and the force grew.

"We need a few more, though," Mosby said. "Mebbe some likely jiggers will happen along. Chuck line ridin' time beginnin'. Keep yore eyes skun, Jim."

Hatfield was keeping them "skun," in more ways than one. He carefully went over the proposed route of the conveyor line, checking the topographical and mechanical difficulties and deciding on sites for the relay engines.

It was natural for him to do so, because, before the murder of his father by wideloopers had sent him into the Rangers, Jim Hatfield had had three years in a famous college of engineering. His interest in the subject had never flagged. He had kept up his studies during the years that followed, and although he had never followed engineering as a profession, he knew more about it than many a man who could write C.E. or B.S. after his name.

Henry Blaine, John Mosby's mining engineer, had been entrusted with the job of constructing the conveyor system, but Hatfield desired to keep tabs on the work, knowing that a mistake in the construction could easily be attendant with future difficulties of magnitude in the successful operation of the extended system, which would be longer than any he had ever had experience with.

He also familiarized himself with the hills about the site of the Silver City mine, and was not favorably impressed with the terrain.

"A reg'lar hole-in-the-wall country," he told Goldy. "A perfect hangout section for gents with shady notions. If Jose Muerta is as smart as he 'pears to be, I wouldn't be surprised if he makes this his nawth-of-the-line headquarters. Well, we'll just get a notion of this up-ended rear part of Creation ourselves."

A couple of weeks after taking employ under Mosby, Hatfield rode west of the mine site along the Tornillo Trail. He rode slowly, his eyes keenly studying the sags and the canyons. He was perhaps ten miles west of the mine when he discovered what he sought and what he had shrewdly suspected existed.

So faint that it would ordinarily escape the notice of the casual traveler, a trail branched off from the Tornillo and dipped sharply down a brush-grown slope, almost paralleling the main trail for a while, then turning south.

It was little more than a tunnel through the high and thick chaparral growth that encroached so closely upon the winding track that at times the branches interlaced overhead. But it showed unmistakable signs of having been recently traveled by a number of horses.

"This is the way those hellions went the night of the mine office robbery," he decided. "This is their short cut to *manana* land, or somewhere else. I've a notion there isn't a foot of this hull border section that yellow-haired hellion doesn't know like the palm of his hand. No wonder he can swoop down on a place and then just seem to vanish into the air."

For more than an hour he followed the track, which again veered to the west. Hatfield found himself riding along the lip of a long, boulder-strewn slope which dropped sharply downward to the floor of a valley. He pulled Goldy to a halt and sat staring into the wide gorge.

Following its course, east to west, were what looked like thin threads of burnished silver.

"That's the C & P railroad line," Hatfield mused.

Perhaps half a hundred yards up the slope from the railroad tracks was a trail that paralleled the one he was riding, a wider trail that vanished around a jutting shoulder of cliff that seemed to practically overhang the railroad. Here, Hatfield noted, the trail would not be more than a score of feet from the C & P right of way.

Hatfield followed, with his eyes, the line of the railroad into the sun-drenched east. He saw, miles distant, a shimmering yellow streak with a dark, feathery plume hanging over it. Both streak and plume were undoubtedly drawing nearer, though the distance was so great as to make their progress barely perceptible. Hatfield knew the yellow streak to be one of C & P's crack passenger trains thundering westward. He idly studied the approaching train, then dropped his gaze back to the trail at the foot of the slope. More by instinct than anything else, he sensed movement in the shadows below.

"Now what in blazes are those jiggers up to down there?" he muttered, staring at the antlike figures busy near the base of the jutting shoulder of rock.

For some minutes he studied with narrowed eyes the activities where the trail veered sharply toward the railroad. Suddenly he stiffened in the saddle, his gaze shot toward the approaching train, now looming large as it roared through the valley. Already his ears could catch the chuckling purr of the great locomotive's exhaust.

He glanced toward the shoulder of rock once more, tightened his grip on the bridle. His face was bleak as chiseled granite, his eyes coldly gray. His voice rang out like a golden trumpet of sound:

"Trail, Goldy, trail! All hell's gonna bust loose down there if we don't get there in time to stop it! Trail!"

Over the lip of the slope went the snorting horse, liking it not at all, but obeying without question his rider's command. Sliding, slipping, staggering, he plowed through the shale and the loose boulders, sending up clouds of dust, starting miniature avalanches, keeping his footing by succeeding miracles of agility and through the skill and strength of the iron grip on his bridle and the supple sway of his rider's body.

TWELVE

The Sunset Flyer was late, and making up time. In the cab of the giant locomotive, old Ad Carnahan bounced about on his seatbox, puffing at a battered corncob pipe and swearing cheerfully at his fireman, Smoky Woods. The while, his keen old eyes scanned the right of way ahead, shifted to the steam gauge needle, wavering against the two hundred pounds pressure mark, glanced back at the twin steel ribbons unfolding beneath the engine's grinding drivers. He surveyed the water glass with a disapproving regard and reached for his injector valve handle. Water gurgled through the intake pipe. Carnahan squinted judiciously at the steam gauge once more.

Smoky Woods also glanced at the steam gauge, hopped to the deck and grabbed his shovel. He flung open the firedoor and baled "black diamonds" into the roaring furnace. Black smoke gushed from the stack in pluming clouds. Woods slammed the firedoor shut and studied the gauge. The needle, which had begun to drop as cold water poured into the boiler, slowly rose again. Smoky grunted, and wiped his streaming face with the sleeve of his jumper. Old Ad widened the throttle a trifle, hooked the reverse bar up another notch toward the center of the quadrant.

145

The chuckling purr of the exhaust deepened, the flashing siderods and the grinding drivers sang to a quickened tempo.

"You're gonna take one of them curves in a straight line if you don't watch out," Smoky bawled above the uproar of the flying engine.

"Save time that way," was Wild Ad's imperturbable reply.

Smoky grunted profanity under his breath, and bent to the shovel once more. Carnahan stared ahead with puckered lids.

"Curve'll be on your side in a minute," he called warningly to the tallowpot.

Smoky Woods snorted, slid the shovel firmly under the coal trickling through the tender gates, and hopped to the seatbox, straining his eyes ahead as the locomotive reeled as it left the tangent and ground the flanges against the beginning of the wide curve around a shoulder of rock a few hundred yards distant. Suddenly he stiffened, gripped the window ledge with both hands and stared ahead.

"Look out, Ad!" he screamed. "The hull cliff's comin' down on the track!"

Instantly old Ad reacted to the warning. He slammed the throttle shut, gripped the air brake handle, and "wiped the gauge"!

Air screamed through the port as the exhaust knifed off. The brake shoes clanged against the tires, the great engine leaped and bucked like a living thing. From behind came the howl of tortured metal and a prodigious slamming and banging of couplers. Then the hundreds of tons of steel which were the long passenger train crashed against the tender drawbar. The locomotive shot forward as if shoved by a mighty hand, brakes screaming, drivers bellowing their protest.

Madly old Ad fought to save his train. Back came the reverse bar, wide open jerked the throttle. With a maddened shriek of abused machinery, the great drivers revolved backward, spun wildly as the tires slipped on the rails, the exhaust roaring and thundering. Old Ad twirled the sand blowers wide open. Sand gushed under the spinning drivers. They ground, screeched, gripped the rails. Then again came that tremendous shove of the speeding coaches, hurtling the locomotive forward on slipping tires. Showers of sparks flew out on either side. The engine rocked and swayed wildly.

"You can't do it, Ad!" shrieked Smoky. "Leave 'er! She's gonna hit!"

"This side!" bellowed the engineer as he leaped to the gangway and stood gripping the grab irons in the narrow opening between engine cab and tender. "This side, Smoky! She'll turn over on your side—low side of the curve!"

Smoky Woods streaked across the cab, leaped to the engineer's window and poised on hands and knees. An instant later his body shot from the cab like a projectile. He cleared the eastbound tracks and hit the slope of the earth embankment with a muffled thud. Carnahan jumped at the same moment, barely cleared the tie ends. Together, fireman and engineer plowed down the embankment in a smother of dust.

With a thundering crash, the locomotive hit the mass of splintered stone piled high across the tracks. It leaped high into the air, twisted like a jumping frog and spun over on its side. Fire and scalding water flew in all directions. Clouds of smoke billowed up. Steam pouring from the intake of a torn-off cylinder added its raucous bellow to the pandemonium of terrifying sound. Back along the wrecked train sounded the screams of cut and bruised and terror-stricken passengers.

The express car, next to the engine, was derailed. The glass of its windows was shattered to fragments. Its side doors were wrenched wide open by the force of the impact, and jammed in their slots.

Out of the growth that flanked the right of way streamed yelling figures, guns spouting flame and spatting bullets against the steel sides of the express car. Inside the car sounded startled shouts, then a crackle of answering shots.

One of the train wreckers gave a howl of pain and pitched forward onto his face to lie moaning and retching, his life ebbing swiftly from a bullet hole beneath his heart. The others, with curses of rage, dived for cover. Their guns continued to crack, sending a shower of slugs through the doors and windows of the express car. The messengers crouched inside raked the growth with bullets.

Something soared through the air, leaving a train of smoke spurting behind it. It vanished through the open door of the express car. An instant later the coach rocked and swayed to a booming explosion. Smoke gushed out the doors and windows. The firing within abruptly ceased. Again the owlhoots left the brush and ran forward. And again they were met with hissing lead. A tall young man with a short black beard was firing at them from the front vestibule of the coach directly behind the derailed express car.

Yells and curses answered this new attack, and once more the outlaws fled for cover. Their attacker, partially sheltered by the steel sides and end of the vestibule, crouched low and answered them shot for shot.

But the bandits were crawling through the brush and would quickly outflank him, getting into position to fire directly through the openings left by the shattered glass in the side doors of the vestibule. In another minute or two his position would be untenable.

And then all hell hit the owlhoots from the rear. Racing down the steep slope in a shower of dislodged stones and a cloud of dust came a great golden horse. He hit the trail above the right of way on bunched hoofs, reeled, staggered, came to a halt, blowing and snorting. His tall rider streaked hands to the butts of long black guns. The guns spat flame. Startled yells and a scream of pain came from the brush. The man in the vestibule let out an exultant whoop and raked the growth with his fire. Again the guns on the trail roared, and again a shriek of agony knifed through the turmoil.

The train wreckers had enough of it. The growth agitated wildly as they tore through it toward the shattered cliff. Leaping and scrambling, they swarmed over the splintered stone that heaped the track, nearly a dozen of them, and dived out of sight.

Jim Hatfield whirled Goldy's head, but instantly realized that the trail was blocked by a jumbled mass of broken rock that no horse could clamber over. He swung to the ground, sliding his heavy Winchester from the saddle boot, and raced down the trail. But by the time he had clawed his way over the obstruction and around the shoulder of cliff, the owlhoots had vanished. Above the diminishing grumble of the escaping steam he heard the click of racing hoofs, swiftly fading into the distance. He stared after the sound for a moment, glanced back at Goldy, and shook his head.

"Mighty slim chance of even you catching them up, feller," he said. "And if we did, there'd be a mighty *good* chance of not knowing what to do with them when we caught them. Nine or ten of the hellions, and odds like that are a mite lopsided. Besides," he added with grim remembrance of the night at the Silver City mine, "while we were hightailin' after them, some of the bunch would like as not cut away and snuk back here to finish the job. Wouldn't put it past 'em, if they're the same outfit what robbed the mine, and they're mighty liable to be. Must be something mighty wuth while in that express car, and it'll stand a mite of watching."

He scrambled down the slope to the right of way. Passengers were streaming from the coaches. The engineer, bruised and battered, but apparently in pretty good shape, was just climbing into the express car. The fireman was scrambling over the piled stone to flag the eastbound track, which was also blocked. The bearded young man was bending over the body of the owlhoot who had fallen to the first volley from the express car. He glanced up as Hatfield approached and his teeth flashed white through his beard in a friendly grin.

"Feller," he declared warmly, "I never was quite so glad to see anybody as I was to see you comin' down that sag. I was figgerin' my number was up for sure."

"Wish I coulda got here sooner," Hatfield replied. "Then mebbe I could have stopped this before it happened. I saw the hellions from the trail up top the sag. Couldn't figger at fust what they were up to. By the time I caught on, it was too late to stop either the train or the dynamite they'd planted in the cliff."

"Well," said the other, "they're two short, anyhow. This one and another one over there in the brush that you downed. I figger yuh nicked another one, mebbe a couple, judgin' from the yellin'. This is an ornery lookin' sidewinder, ain't he? The one in the brush is of the same breed."

Hatfield peered into the swarthy face of the dead owlhoot.

"Full blood Yaqui, I'd say," he decided. "Yuh say the other is the same?"

"Other one might have a dash of white blood, I figger," replied the bearded man.

Hatfield nodded, his black brows drawing together thoughtfully. He glanced at the derailed coach.

"Scairt those pore devils in the express car are done for," he remarked. "S'pose we go and see."

The other nodded agreement and together they clambered into the coach, the inside of which was badly turn up by the explosion of the dynamite the wreckers had tossed into it.

They found one messenger unconscious with a badly gashed scalp. His companion was bruised and cut and had a broken arm, but Hatfield decided that neither was fatally injured.

"And they didn't get the shipment, thanks to you two fellers," the messenger gasped as Hatfield splinted and bandaged his fractured arm.

"Big shipment?" the Ranger asked.

"Damn big," panted the messenger, swabbing the sweat drops from his face with his uninjured hand. "Quarter of a million in gold coin—goin' to an Arizona bank.

"But what I can't figger," he added querulously, "is how those skunks learned the shipment was on this train. Supposed to be a secret known only to the officials of the bank and the express company."

"Mebbe they were just taking a gamble on you having something wuth lifting," Hatfield suggested.

"Mebbe," the messenger grunted dubiously, "but it would be a hell of a chance to take, with a dozen through trains passin' over the line every twenty-four hours. Nope, I don't think so. I figger there musta been a leak somewhere and the information reached the skunks some way. There'll be hell at headquarters about this."

Hatfield made no further comment, but again the concentration furrow deepened between his brows, and his green eyes were thoughtful.

"There, that'll hold yuh till yuh get to the hospital," he told the messenger. "Reckon we'd better help the engineer tie up yore pardner's head now. I see he's getting his senses back. Then we'll see if any of the passengers are bad hurt."

His fears on that score were relieved, however, by the conductor, who at that moment climbed into the coach.

"Shook up bad, a few bruises, and some cuts from flyin' glass," he replied to Hatfield's question. "Mostly scairt. Nothin' pertickler bad."

A deep-toned whistle sounded, from the west.

"That'll be the Continent Limited, eastbound," said the conductor. "They'll highball a man back to that little local stop about three miles farther on and wire Radford, twenty miles to the west, our next stop. They got a wreck train at Radford. They'll clean up this mess in a jiffy. Sure has got the hull system tied up proper, though. The second section of the Flyer is standin' behind us right now, and I reckon there's trains lined up all the way to Alamita. Yeah, she's a mess."

"Radford," remarked the young man, "that's where I aimed to stop off. Figgered I might be able to tie onto a job of ridin' on one of the spreads nawth of Radford."

Hatfield eyed the speaker contemplatively, noting his clear hazel eyes that had a straightforward look to them, and the clean, firm lines of chin and jaw that the growth of beard did not wholly conceal.

"Might be able to tie yuh onto a job over Alamita way, feller," he suggested.

The other regarded him with an almost startled look.

"Alamita," he repeated. He raised a hand and scratched at the growth on his cheek. Hatfield's eyes narrowed a trifle at the gesture, but he merely nodded.

"Alamita," the other said again, his fingers still digging at the beard. "Job of ridin'?"

"Not exactly chambermaidin' cows," Hatfield admitted. "But there's considerable riding tied onto it, all right, and the pay's quite a mite better than punching cows dishes out."

Briefly he explained the duties of the mine patrol. The other listened, appeared to consider, fingering his beard meditatively, then suddenly arriving at a decision.

"Okay," he agreed, "reckon I could do wuss than give it a whirl. My name's W-Walt— Smith."

Hatfield noticed his momentary hesitation over the name, but proffered no comment. He supplied his own name, and they shook hands.

"How'll I get to the mines from here?" Smith asked.

Hatfield glanced up to the trail. "Old Goldy will carry double," he said, "and I reckon yuh can stand it behind a saddle for that distance. We'll get yuh a horse and an outfit at the mine."

"Fine," Smith agreed. "I'll get my warbag—it's back in the coach."

He strode off to the train and reappeared a few minutes later bearing a battered "turkey." He and Hatfield climbed the slope to the trail.

When they reached the crest, Smith paused to stare back musingly at the wrecked train.

"Sure didn't figger on gettin' off here," he said, "but then I've been getting off at a lot of places I hadn't figgered on durin' the past few years." He chuckled mirthlessly, his eyes somber.

"Funny," he remarked, "I'm right back where I started from—a job of ridin' for wages. Had other notions when I started off on my own a few years ago. Figgered on mowin' the world down, but found it mighty tough cuttin'. Dreamed of doin' big things, only I didn't do 'em."

"Something to have dreamed," Hatfield said quietly.

"More to have done things," Smith replied, his bearded lips twisting in a smile of self-derision.

"Something to have dreamed," the Ranger repeated. "Pertickler," he added, "if yuh finally get to make the dreams come true. You got a heap of time ahead of yuh, feller, or should have. Keep walking after yore dreams, and some day mebbe yuh'll catch up with them."

"Mebbe," Smith grunted morosely, "but I'm sure a long way behind right now."

THIRTEEN

Goldy bore his double load to the mine without difficulty. Once there, Smith was soon fitted with a horse and riding gear and introduced to his fellow guards. Hatfield had a number of details to attend to, but early the following afternoon he and Smith headed for Alamita.

"I've a notion the sheriff will wanta hear fust hand from us about what we had to do in that shindig at the wreck," Hatfield explained to the new recruit. "I've a notion he's gonna have something to say on his own account. He's sorta on the prod against everything of late. Can't hardly blame him, though. Things haven't been going over good in his bailiwick."

Salty Craig Wilson was plenty on the prod.

"Feller," he told Hatfield, "I've a notion yuh're one of them there bad luck pieces a jigger gets inter his poke every now and then. Ever since you lit here, things have been gettin' wuss and wuss. The way you can hop outa one hell raisin' inter another is a caution to cats!

"Not that yuh didn't do a purty good chore yesterday," he admitted grudgingly. "And that goes for you, too, Smith. Reckon if it hadn't been for you fellers, them hellions woulda got away with that shipment. Doin' in them two 'breed sidewinders was fust rate. That's two I won't hafta bother about hangin'. Didn't notice anythin' about them that would serve to tie 'em up with somebody, did yuh?"

"Nothing in their pockets, nothing out of the ord'nary about their rigs," Hatfield replied. "The rest of the bunch took their horses along with them when they hightailed."

Sheriff Wilson swore wearily. "Oh, it was the Muerta outfit, all right," he declared. "Yaqui breeds—the sort what trails along after that yaller-haired sidewinder. But what I'd like to know is how did they figger which train to hit? That's what the express company and the bank officials over East would like to know, too. No, John Mosby isn't in town. Rode up to his spread this mawnin'."

Smith had some purchases to make, and after arranging to meet him later, Hatfield sauntered down the street to the Greasy Sack.

Pecos Rose was standing at the far end of the bar when Hatfield entered, conversing earnestly with a tall man whose eyes gleamed under the low-drawn brim of a black J.B. He had a lean, big-nosed face bronzed with the ruddy sort of bronze that a light complexion acquires when much exposed to wind and weather. His nostrils flared somewhat, lending a fleshy bulk to the big nose, and there were bunches of muscle bulging his cheeks where they touched the jawbone, which served to broaden an otherwise lean countenance. His upper lip was shaded by a small, carefully trimmed black mustache. His hair, which was rather long, was lank and jet black. He wore the funeral garb of a gambler, its dead black relieved only by the snow of his ruffled shirt front. His black boots were polished to mirror-like brightness. No weapons were visible on him, but Hatfield noted a slight bulge to his coat at the left armpit, which decided the Ranger that a gun snugged there in a shoulder holster.

His glance slid over the Lone Wolf's face at his entrance, then apparently dismissed him. His gaze drew back to Pecos Rose and he continued his conversation with her.

After a few more minutes of talk, Pecos Rose shook her head in an undecided manner. The man spoke a word or two further, bowed slightly, turned and left the saloon. The lithe grace of his movement reminded Hatfield of a great cat stalking through tall grass.

Pecos Rose watched his departure, then moved down the bar to pause beside Hatfield. Her eyes rested on the swinging doors through which the stranger had vanished.

"New man in town," she remarked in her soft, slightly throaty voice. "Name of John Morton. He wants to buy my place, or an interest in it."

"Going to sell?" Hatfield asked.

Pecos Rose hesitated. "I don't know, yet," she admitted frankly. "It's a good paying business, but there are reasons why I'd like to get out of it."

Hatfield was about to comment, when he saw her lips tighten grimly. At the same instant, the tapping of a cane sounded behind him. He glanced over his shoulder and saw Lynn Dawson making his way slowly across the room. Beside him, holding his arm and guiding him through the crowd, was a girl.

She was slight and graceful, with a wealth of ruddy gold hair, wide blue eyes and a piquant, creamily tanned face. She had a straight little nose, the bridge of which was delicately powdered with a few freckles. Her mouth was soft and red, with a dimple just suggested at one corner. She smiled, and her eyes brightened as they rested on Pecos Rose.

"I brought Mr. Dawson in to have dinner with me here," she said brightly.

"Yes," said Pecos Rose.

The girl smiled questioningly at Hatfield, then passed on, guiding the nearly blind man to a small table in a corner. Pecos Rose followed the pair with her eyes.

"Pity that feller's eyes are so bad," Hatfield remarked. "Can't say as I ever saw a handsomer jigger."

"Yes," said Pecos Rose.

Hatfield glanced at her, struck by something in her voice that did not tally with her monosyllabic agreement. But Rose did not amplify her remark.

"The girl work here?" he asked.

"She does not!" Pecos Rose replied emphatically. She hesitated, then added, a trifle grimly:

"That's my daughter. She just got back from college."

Hatfield gazed at the pretty girl with added interest. She was undoubtedly very young, and she seemed decidedly out of place in the Greasy Sack.

"That," said Pecos Rose, "is the reason I want to get out of this business."

Hatfield regarded her a moment. "And what would yuh do then?" he asked curiously.

"There's a ranch over to the northeast of town for sale—joins up with John Mosby's Bar M," Rose replied. "I think I'd buy that. I know considerable about the cow business. Was raised to it."

Hatfield gazed down at her from his great height, in his green eyes was decided approval.

"Ma'am," he said, "under the circumstances, I figger that's a plumb swell notion."

"I think so, too," Pecos Rose agreed. "In fact, I think so enough to do it. When that gambling man, Morton, comes around tomorrow, if he does as he said he would, I'm going to sell out. Let's have a drink on it."

They were having the drink when the doors

swung open and Walt Smith entered hurriedly. He glanced around the room, waved a greeting to Hatfield and started in his direction. Suddenly, however, his gaze rested on the golden-haired girl at the corner table, he half halted in his stride, and apparently forgot all about the Ranger.

And at the same instant the girl glanced up and their eyes met squarely.

Hatfield saw her eyes widen. Her lips parted slightly. Then the silken curtains of her lashes swept down to veil the blue of her eyes. Over her soft cheeks rushed a wave of color. She turned swiftly to Dawson, and began to speak in a breathless sort of way. Dawson's face mirrored bewilderment. He peered at her, raised his head, and Hatfield saw his pale eyes glint behind his glasses.

Walt Smith stumbled, half off balance, then jerked himself erect and moved to join Hatfield, a slightly dazed look in his eyes.

Pecos Rose smiled grimly, and acknowledged Hatfield's introduction of his companion with a nod of her flaming head.

They had a drink together, then Hatfield and Smith left the saloon. The moment they reached the street, the younger man turned excitedly to his companion.

"Who is she?" he demanded.

"Who's who?" Hatfield countered.

"The girl!" exclaimed Smith.

"Yuh mean Pecos Rose?" Hatfield replied innocently. "Why, she owns the place."

"No! No!" bawled Smith. "I mean the girl at the table! Isn't she a wonder!"

"Oh, her," Hatfield replied ungrammatically. "I didn't catch her name, but she's Pecos Rose's daughter."

Smith halted dead in his tracks and glared at the Ranger.

"Why didn't yuh tell me?" he exploded.

"Why didn't yuh ask me?" Hatfield chuckled.

"I'd have played up to her if yuh had," said Smith.

"Why, there was a good lookin' gent with her," Hatfield demurred, "and she looked plumb int'rested in him."

"No, I mean Pecos Rose!" Smith sputtered exasperatedly. "That way I mighta got a chance to meet the daughter."

"Mebbe yuh'll get a chance anyhow," Hatfield comforted. "Take it easy, feller, yore loop's slippin'."

Walt Smith muttered cuss words under his breath and scratched viciously at his beard.

"Anyhow," he declared with conviction, "I'm plumb glad I came to Alamita, after all."

"After all?" Hatfield repeated quietly. "Were yuh figgerin' on coming here in the fust place?"

Smith muttered something unintelligible in his beard, but did not directly reply to the question.

"Let's stop in here for another drink," he suggested, jerking his thumb toward the Anytime's plate glass window.

"Okay, one," Hatfield agreed. "Then we gotta be heading back to the mine."

Hatfield was unusually silent in the course of the ride back to the Silver City, and the concentration furrow was deep between his brows.

"What yuh thinkin' about, Jim?" Smith was at length constrained to ask.

"Eyes," the Lone Wolf replied, with the shadow of a smile.

"Uh-huh, wasn't they wonderful!" Smith enthused. "So big and wide and blue! Never saw such eyes! Glad you noticed 'em, too."

Hatfield smiled sympathetically, but did not comment further.

Several days passed before Hatfield found an opportunity to visit Alamita again. When he arrived there, he heard a startling piece of news. John Mosby was his informant.

"Have yuh heerd the latest?" Mosby squealed indignantly. "That blankety-blank Muerta has set up as an *El Libertador* below the line, and has started a rev'lution against old *El Presidente*. Says he's gonna set up a sep'rate state made outa Chihuahua and Sonora and Sinaloa, with him as the head of the gov'ment. Now what do yuh think of that, Jim?"

Hatfield digested the information. "I think," he

said gravely at length, "that he'll scare the life outa *El Presidente*, and Texas too, mebbe, before he's finished with them."

Mosby stared. He had already come to greatly respect Jim Hatfield's ability and judgment, but this was going a mite strong.

"Yuh mean to say," he demanded, "that that half-peso bandit has a chance to get by with what he sets up to do?"

"Yes," Hatfield replied quietly, "if he isn't stopped short off."

"But—but," exclaimed Mosby in bewilderment, "what makes yuh believe that—that nonsense?"

"I'm not at all sure it's nonsense, John," Hatfield countered. "Yuh see, folks down below the line are beginning to get a mite of a glimmering of light on *El Presidente*'s government. They're beginning to see things as they really are. In other words, they're beginning to *think*. John, there's a big country the other side of the river—a big country, and one of the richest, naturally, in the world. Down there is one of the finest, grandest bits of earth on this hemisphere. Folks don't realize it yet—don't realize what it is going to become. It has everything necessary to make a powerful, prosperous, happy country. Right now it isn't any of those things, and the folks who live down there are at last beginning to see that for centuries they have been done out of what is rightly theirs. Right now they're stirring—they're ripe for a change. It's a condition that makes for opportunity for gents of the Muerta stamp. It's been tried before, and once or twice it almost succeeded, only the time wasn't just right. There was the Maximilian conquest. It was mighty nigh put over. Then there was William Walker, who came to the end of his twine filibustering down in Nicaragua. The gray-eyed man of destiny, they called him. He set up the Republic of Lower California and Sonora and was going sorta strong for a while; but like Maximilian, he was an outsider, and the folks below the line wouldn't back him up and kicked him and his gang out. And there was Joaquin Murietta, the California bandit leader, and Juan Flores, and others. And now we have Jose Muerta, and I figger he's about the most dangerous of the lot."

"But, after all," objected Mosby, "what difference does it make to us folks up here what he does down there?"

Hatfield smiled slightly, but his eyes were somber.

"That's a question," he said, "that sooner or later usually makes for hard answering by folks who ask it. John, we hafta live with our neighbors, and it will make a heap of a big difference to us whether they are good neighbors or bad. If Muerta gets by with what he's starting with Sonora and Sinaloa and Chihuahua, it's only a matter of time until he has all Mexico, and

Muerta would make a mighty bad neighbor for Texas."

Mosby tugged viciously at his mustache. "I didn't credit that raidin' hellion with havin' enough brains to put over anythin' like that," he declared, "and what's more, I don't know."

"Mebbe yuh're right there," Hatfield conceded, "but there's another angle to which I've been giving some serious thought of late. Muerta may not have the savvy to put such a thing over. But there may be *somebody back of Muerta who does have the brains needed.* Somebody who hasn't come to the front yet. Somebody who stays behind in the shadows and pulls the strings, and who will loom up big when the right time comes. That's a possibility we hafta take inter consideration."

He paused a moment, his eyes thoughtful.

"John," he said, "did yuh ever stop to think that Muerta doesn't run true to form, that he isn't like the average run of border bandits? Usually they make a good haul or two and then drift off to enjoy what they got, and most often end up drinking themselves to death or getting killed in a brawl. Muerta is different. He's been kicking up hell here and south of the line for the past coupla years—working mostly the other side of the river and coming up here only during recent months, no doubt because the pickings are better up here. He's made some mighty big hauls. He's glommed onto more pesos than the average border bandit would know what to do with, even how to count. But he doesn't stop. He keeps right on, going in for something bigger each time. That train robbery would have netted him a quarter of a million dollars, if he had got away with it. He seems to want a pow'ful lot of money for something or other. What yuh just told me ties up with the way he's been acting. Looks like he, or somebody who is using him, has been amassing money over quite a spell for some definite purpose. We're beginning to get a notion as to what that purpose might be."

"But if he goes in for revolutin' down there, anyhow, we'll be finished with him up here," contended Mosby.

Hatfield slowly shook his head.

"There yuh're plumb wrong, John," he replied gravely. "To put over what he has in mind, he'll need more money, lots of it. He can't get it down there. He'll hafta cross the river for it. No, we're not through with *Don* Jose, not by a jugful."

Mosby swore querulously, his brows knitted.

"Jim," he complained, "yuh done got me worried. What the hell do yuh think is gonna happen?"

"Plenty, if Muerta isn't pulled up short," he replied. His face was bleak as he looked into the future with eyes of vision.

"John," he said, "things are gonna change,

pertickler in that big, rich country below the line. There's a wind rising, a wind that will topple institutions and scatter old things and customs as if they were chaff. Sooner or later a man will rise up down there who will sweep *El Presidente* and all that he and his class stand for out of existence. There'll be blood and toil and sweat and tears for the people down there, but out of all that will come a new Mexico, a great country, strong and progressive, with only her people's will to rule her from the yellow waters of the Rio Grande to the blue mountains of Guatemala. That country will be our friend, our good neighbor—if the man who rises up is the right man, if the men who follow him are the right men. I do not think that Jose Muerta, or anybody associated with him, is the right man. If Muerta succeeds in what he has set out to do, there will be a government below the line that will hate us, and that will teach its people to hate us, and, as I said before, the time will come when they are a strong people, big enough to make us plenty of trouble, and Texas will be the focus of wrath. *Our* lot will be blood, sweat and tears—if Muerta isn't stopped."

Old John Mosby stared at the towering form and sternly handsome face of the Lone Wolf.

"Jim," he said slowly, "yuh're a strange feller— for a wanderin' cowboy!"

"Yes," Hatfield smiled agreement, "for a wandering cowboy!"

FOURTEEN

Two days after his conversation with Mosby, Hatfield had a run-in with Henry Blaine, the engineer charged with the construction of the conveyor system. He was riding slowly along the survey line, checking the proposed sites of the towers from which the overhead cables would be suspended.

As he progressed farther and farther along the route, his eyes grew puzzled. Finally he pulled Goldy to a halt, hooked one leg comfortably over the saddle horn and drew from his pocket a notebook and a pencil. He covered a couple of leaves of the book with symbols and figures, thoughtfully considered the results, and checked the figures again with great care. For some minutes he sat gazing at the survey line, his eyes subtly changing color until they were coldly gray as the granite cliffs. His mouth was set in grim lines when he gathered up the reins and rode swiftly to where he knew he would find the engineer.

Blaine, a thin, nervous man with a magnificently shaped head but with uncertain eyes and mouth, who was directing the operations of some workmen, greeted him with effusive cordiality. Hatfield swung to the ground and launched into the matter at hand without preamble.

170

"Blaine," he said, "yuh've made a serious mistake."

The engineer bridled. "What are you talking about?" he demanded.

"The sites for the cable towers," Hatfield told him. "They're spaced wrong."

Blaine began to bluster indignantly. "What do you mean, wrong?" he demanded. "Don't you think I know my business? Who are you to tell me how this work should be done?"

"That's beside the point, Blaine," Hatfield said quietly. "The fact remains you have made a bad mistake. What's so terrible about that?" he added quickly as Blaine endeavored to cut in. "Engineers have made mistakes before now. Everybody makes them. Your towers are spaced too far apart. The distance they are spaced, the cable sag will be so great that you will never be able to haul the empty buckets back up the mountain. What's more, your loaded conveyors coming down will bog on that slack. Their velocity will not be great enough to take them up the sag and over the hump where the cables are suspended from the towers."

"I tell you—" Blaine began to bawl. Hatfield's voice cut through his yammer like a silver blade through clabber:

"Shut up, and wait until I have done. I'm not guessing. I'm telling you facts. Hand me yore pad and pencil."

With the full force of the Lone Wolf's eyes upon him, Blaine stopped talking and obeyed. Hatfield covered a sheet of the pad with swift figures. He handed the result to the engineer.

"Still figure yuh haven't made a mistake?" he asked softly.

Blaine took the pad, with a hand that trembled slightly. In his eyes was an expression of anger and bafflement. He checked the figures, wet his lips with the tip of his tongue. He drew a deep breath. Then abruptly his face cleared and he essayed a smile.

"Hatfield," he exclaimed with bluff heartiness, "you're right! I did make a mistake—checked my grade figures wrong. Yes, I made a mistake, and I hope I'm a big enough man to thank you for pointing it out to me. You have saved me a lot of trouble and an awful row with the Old Man. Mosby would have hit the ceiling if this hadn't been caught in time. I'll rectify this right away."

Hatfield nodded. "Just figgered you'd like to know about it, in time," he agreed.

"That's right," Blaine declared. He glanced at the Ranger curiously. "You seem to know considerable about such matters, for a cowhand," he remarked.

"I helped install a conveyor system once," Hatfield evaded. "Well, be seeing yuh. Got to get back to the mine."

Blaine watched him ride off the way he had

come, and the fury was back in his nervous eyes.

"Helped install a conveyor system once, eh?" he repeated the Ranger's words. "And got a thorough grounding in the principles of higher mathematics while doing it! This calls for some action."

As soon as Hatfield was out of sight around a bend, he hurried to where his own horse was tethered and, after a few words of instruction to the gang of workmen, mounted and rode swiftly toward Alamita, muttering under his breath and, from time to time, glancing nervously over his shoulder.

John Mosby had installed a commodious and comfortable bunkhouse at the mine site for his guard patrol. Hatfield was seated by a window, smoking thoughtfully, when Walt Smith came hurrying in.

"Her name's Helen!" he exclaimed. "Ain't that a plumb purty name?"

Hatfield glanced up absently. "Who's named Helen?" he wanted to know.

"Why, her—Helen Marcy—Pecos Rose's daughter. I learned a lot of things about her, too. Her father got hisself killed in a stampede about seven years ago. Her mother bought the Greasy Sack from a jigger named Bofkins, who was drinkin' so much of the likker there wasn't any left for the customers. She ran the place right, made money, and put Helen through school and college. Now she's got outa the saloon business, because of Helen, and bought the Fiddle-Back spread, which has been for sale since old Arn Hale died last year. It's just south and east of my—of the Bar M. Just as soon as I can get an afternoon off, I wanta ride over there. Mebbe I can give 'em some advice about runnin' the spread. Can't get to see the girl in town. That jigger Dawson is allus hangin' around her when she's there. I've a notion she feels sorry for him because his eyes are so bad."

"Could be," Hatfield admitted. He stared out of the window thoughtfully, returned his regard to Smith.

"I've a notion yuh might make more of a hit with her if yuh mowed that brush off yore face," he advised. "A feller as young as you hasn't any business hiding behind such a chaparral thicket."

Smith looked startled, instinctively raised his hand to scratch at his cheeks.

"I—I been wearin' it so long I sorta got used to it—would be—be sorta lost without it," he muttered.

"Reckon that's so," Hatfield agreed, "for a feller what's been wearing whiskers a long time."

As Smith hurried out to wash up before chuck time, Hatfield gazed after him thoughtfully.

"Funny," he mused. "Every now and then I get a feeling that I've seen that jigger somewhere before—or mebbe he reminds me of somebody else. But who? Been wearing whiskers a long time, eh? But not long enough for them to stop itching. Well, mebbe dif'rent folks measure time sorta dif'rent."

The following day, Hatfield rode to town. On inquiring at the Anytime, he learned that John Mosby was at his spread.

"Figgers on stayin' overnight," said his informant, the head bartender.

Hatfield requested information as to how to get to the Bar M. The barkeep supplied it, in detail. As Hatfield walked toward the door, the bartender, in afterthought, asked a question of Lynn Dawson, the bank and mine manager, who was sipping a drink at a nearby table.

"Mr. Dawson jest said John will be back in town by noon t'morrer," the barkeep called to Hatfield.

"I wanta be at the mine again by noon tomorrow," Hatfield called back as he reached the door. "I'll just ride out to the spread and back to town tonight. Had oughta make it there and back by midnight."

Intent eyes followed his progress as he passed out the door.

Before riding for the ranch, Hatfield entered the Greasy Sack, being curious to see how the new owner was making out.

John Morton was standing at the far end of the bar, in Pecos Rose's accustomed place. He was immaculately groomed, even to his black Stetson, which was drawn low over his eyes.

As Hatfield sipped his drink and regarded him curiously, a waiter hurried past Morton with a loaded tray, which he started to place on a nearby table.

Morton suddenly threw up his head, gestured peremptorily to the right and barked an order. The waiter hesitated, then turned and deposited the tray on another table.

Hatfield's black brows drew together. "Funny," he mused, "right then made the second time in two days I've had the feeling I've seen a jigger some place before; but for the life of me I can't tell where or under what circumstances. Am I going loco or something?"

He continued to consider Morton thoughtfully, but the elusive familiarity failed to resolve itself into anything definite. At length, with a shrug of his broad shoulders, he finished his drink and left the saloon.

Hatfield located the Bar M ranch house without difficulty, arriving there shortly before sundown. Cros Cottle, Mosby's foreman, greeted him from the porch as he rode into the yard.

"John's out back somewhere," Cottle announced. "I'll send a wrangler to look for him. Come on in and take a load off yore feet."

He led the way into the main living room of the ranch house, which, Hatfield noted, was commodious and comfortably furnished. It gave an impression of considerable luxury combined with the careless untidiness of the bachelor. He took the chair Cottle motioned him to, and rolled a cigarette. Cottle proceeded to fill his pipe.

"Was over to the Fiddle-Back to visit with our new neighbors," Cottle announced, blowing out a cloud of smoke. "Lynn Dawson was there."

This bit of information, though of interest, Hatfield did not seem to feel required an answer.

"Rose don't like Dawson," Cottle remarked.

"Why not?" Hatfield asked.

"She didn't give no reasons," Cottle returned. "Rose ain't much at givin' reasons for anythin', but she don't. She has a way of settin' her mouth when she looks at a jigger she don't like."

Hatfield nodded, but proffered no further comment. He glanced about the room. His attention was caught by a large photograph on the mantel over the big fireplace.

It was a picture of a good looking, dark-haired youngster with a lean face and smiling eyes.

Cottle noticed the direction of his regard.

"That's Wade Mosby, John's kid," he said.

"That so?" Hatfield replied. "Don't recall seeing him around."

"He ain't around," Cottle explained. "Ain't been around for the past five years. Him and John had a row and he trailed off."

"How was that?" Hatfield wanted to know.

177

"Him and John couldn't hit it off as to what he'd do, when he come back from school," replied Cottle. "John wanted him to go inter the bank and learn the business, but Wade had other notions. Wanted to light out on his own. John couldn't see it that way and laid the law down. Wade is the spittin' image of his mother, who died right after he was born, but he's got a mite of John's mulishness, I reckon. He trailed his rope."

Hatfield smoked in sympathetic silence.

"But I reckon as the years went by, John learned that blood's thicker'n water," Cottle resumed. "I've a mighty good notion he'd give everythin' he owns to know the kid is alive and well. Yuh could never get him to admit it, but if the kid came back, John would make him plumb welcome, even if he come barefoot and in rags."

The Lone Wolf's stern mouth was wonderfully tender, and there was a warm light in his strangely colored eyes as he gazed at the picture on the mantel.

" 'For this my son was dead, and is alive again; he was lost, and is found,' " he quoted softly.

"Eh? What's that?" asked Cottle.

"Yuh'll find it in the Bible—Book of St. Luke, fifteenth chapter, I believe," Hatfield replied smilingly. "It's a nice story, Cros—yuh oughta read it."

Before the puzzled Cottle could reply, the door opened and John Mosby stumped in.

"Cros," he said, "yuh better go and look over that string they just druv inter the pasture. Check what yuh figger we oughta cut out for saddle hosses. Howdy, Hatfield, what's on *yore* mind?"

Hatfield did not immediately reply after Cottle's departure. He was contemplating the picture on the mantel.

"Cros just told me that's a picture of yore son," he remarked. "Didn't know yuh have a son."

"I *had* one," Mosby corrected. "Haven't seed hair or hide of him for more'n five years. He was a wild young hellion. Would go his own way, for all I could do to stop him. Wanted to join the confounded Rangers. Wanted to make his own way. Said he wanted to see the world and do some livin'. Hrumph!"

"Just animal spirits, the chances are," Hatfield comforted.

"Another name for the devil," grunted Mosby; "he's the animal part of us I was brought up to believe. What did yuh wanta see me about, Jim?"

"John," Hatfield replied, "what is the horsepower of the relay engines yuh ordered for the conveyor system?"

"Tell yuh in a minute," said Mosby, getting to his feet and ambling over to his big desk in the corner. He rummaged among some papers in a drawer, drew one out, glanced at it and named a figure.

"John," Hatfield said, "cancel that order by wire, right away. The engines are too light for the job."

"But—but," expostulated Mosby in bewildered tones, "that's the horsepower Henry Blaine recommended. Blaine had oughta know what he is about."

"John," Hatfield told him, "if yuh install those engines, yuh'll just have to tear them out and replace them with heavier ones. That will mean plenty of expense, and, which is more important, plenty of delay. I'll try to explain it to yuh. You know horses and what they can handle. I'll try to explain it in terms of horses."

He crossed to the desk, sat down beside Mosby and began placing figures and diagrams on a sheet of paper, patiently explaining each step in minute detail. Mosby's brows knotted with mental effort. He peered at the figures, asked questions. Gradually his face cleared, and the querulous look in his eyes was replaced by one of understanding, and anger.

"Jim," he said, "I ain't got much eddication, but the way you manage to put it, I can see it. By gosh, yuh're right, or I'm an Injun. Now how in blazes did Blaine come to tangle his twine like that? Of all the dadblamed dumb things to do! I'll—"

"Perhaps," Hatfield interrupted quietly, "Blaine is not as familiar with the grade problems of this section as he might be. Reckon that could be it."

"He's s'posed to be a fust rate engineer," complained Mosby. "Lynn Dawson got him from a company that gave him the very best of recommendations. I'll be dadblamed if I can understand it! Okay, Jim, I'll send that wire changin' the order as soon as I get to town t'morrer afternoon."

"Had oughta be sent right away," Hatfield demurred. "Write it out and I'll send it tonight, when I get to town. We'll be lucky if the shipment hasn't been started already."

"Figgered yuh'd be stayin' here for the night."

"I want to be at the mine tomorrow morning," Hatfield pointed out. "I'd intended riding back to town tonight. And that wire shouldn't be delayed. Here's the horsepower yuh'll need."

He wrote the figure on the paper. Mosby nodded, and with Hatfield's assistance composed the message to the machinery company. Hatfield folded it and placed it in his pocket.

"I'll take care of it fust thing when I hit town," he promised. "The telegraph office at the railroad station is open all night."

After s'roundin' a sizeable helpin' of chuck, Hatfield headed back for Alamita. The night was very clear, the sky thickly powdered with stars. The visibility was fairly good and Hatfield could see a long way across the rolling rangeland. His glance strayed with interest to the east, where the Fiddle-Back, the spread Pecos Rose had lately purchased, was located. He could see, diagonaling toward the Alamita trail he was riding, a second trail that led off across the Bar M to the Fiddle-Back. Perhaps a mile to his left the side trail climbed a ridge to vanish over the crest.

As Hatfield gazed in that direction, suddenly a horseman seemed to float up against the star-burned sky like a mannikin manipulated against a lighted screen by strings. A second emerged noiselessly from behind the hilltop. A third mysteriously materialized. This continued until nearly a dozen riders had risen ghostlike against the sky from the nether shadows. Silently as shades, they drifted down the trail that veered at a wide angle toward the one Hatfield was riding.

Hatfield watched the approach of these phantom horsemen with interest. He estimated that, at their present rate of progress, they should reach the forks of the trail not far behind his own arrival at the point.

The distance was too great, the light too dim, for him to make out features, but it seemed to him that their faces were turned in his direction. A moment later their pace had visibly accelerated.

Hatfield's brows drew together. There was something sinister about these ghostly riders of the night.

"Begins to look like they're making a point to get to the forks before I do," he mused. "If I can see them, the chances are good that they can see me. Now, I wonder?"

The terrain between the two trails was rocky and broken to such an extent that it was not practical for the mysterious riders to cut across the prairie to the Alamita trail. They must follow their own track to the forks.

Hatfield spoke to Goldy. Instantly the great sorrel lengthened his stride. Studying the distant riders, the Ranger quickly concluded that they had also increased their speed.

"Get goin', feller," he told the golden horse. "This is getting interesting."

Within very few minutes, he was convinced that the band was racing to beat him to the forks. His voice rang out, urgent, imperative:

"Trail, Goldy! Trail!"

At that word of command, the sorrel extended himself. His powerful legs drove backward like steel pistons, his irons drumming the surface of the trail. He stretched his glossy neck, blew through his nostrils, and seemed to literally pour his long body over the ground.

Hatfield continued to stare into the shadowy east.

"No doubt about it now," he muttered. "Those jiggers have got a plumb pressin' interest in us. One gent is showing his dust to the rest—way out ahead. That black he's forkin' is a beauty!"

The distance between the two trails was steadily lessening. The mile which had separated them had shrunk to three quarters. Soon it was a half as the point of the angle drew nearer. Glancing ahead, Hatfield saw that, a few hundred yards farther on, a low, rocky and broken ridge began between the trails, rendering them invisible one from the other to almost the point of contact. Swiftly he considered the advisability, once out of sight of the mysterious horsemen, of turning Goldy and riding back again the way he had come; but he decided against it. He was extremely anxious to reach Alamita as soon as possible and besides there was a chance that others of the band might be riding the trail behind him. In which case, were their object really sinister, he would find himself cornered. He cast a final glance at the horsemen before the ridge intervened.

"We're well ahead of the main bunch," he muttered, "and better'n holding our own with that jigger out in front. Reckon it's wuth taking a chance. Sift sand, jughead!"

Goldy "sifted." Nostrils flaring red, eyes rolling, his glorious black mane tossing in the wind of his passing, he thundered down the trail. The ridge bulked solidly on his left. To the right was more broken ground, a jumble of sags and swales.

Directly ahead the ridge curved. Another

moment and it petered out abruptly. And just beyond were the forks of the trail.

As Goldy flashed past the forks, Hatfield heard a drumming of hoofs. Glancing to the right, he saw the great black horse and its rider storming toward him and less than two hundred yards distant. The sky had filmed slightly in the last quarter of an hour and the visibility had appreciably diminished. The approaching horseman was a vague and distorted shadow looming gigantic in the gloom.

A spurt of flame shot from the shadow. Hatfield felt something pluck at his sleeve like an urgent hand. A second bullet grazed his cheek, stinging out drops of blood. A third twitched his hat.

"Blazes! that's shootin'!" he muttered. Leaning over, he slid his heavy Winchester from where it snugged in the saddle boot under his left thigh. He twisted in the saddle and glanced back.

The pursuing horseman had just veered into the Alamita trail. He was coming like the wind. Again that spurt of reddish flame, and again the lethal breath of a rifle slug fanning the Ranger's face.

Hatfield called to Goldy. Instantly the sorrel changed his racing stride to a smooth running walk. Hatfield turned still more, clamped the stock of the rifle against his shoulder. His cold eyes glanced along the sights. His finger squeezed the trigger. The Winchester bucked in his grasp. The crash of the report rang in his ears.

Again he fired, and again, and again.

The black horse seemed to halt in full stride. He reared high, his front hoofs pawing the air, spun over on his side, hurling his rider from the saddle like a stone from a sling.

Hatfield lowered his rifle, seized the bridle and instinctively tightened the curb. But at that instant the rest of the pursuers burst into the trail, yelling and shooting.

Hatfield loosened his grip, his voice rang out, and Goldy raced ahead.

"Odds too big now," he muttered, bending low in the saddle as lead stormed and hissed around him. He slid the rifle back into the boot and devoted his entire attention to getting all possible speed from his mount.

The owlhoots were thundering in pursuit, but Goldy steadily drew away from them. Soon no slugs were coming close. Another moment and Hatfield ceased to hear the crack of the rifles behind. Ten minutes later, as Goldy breasted the crest of a long rise, he glanced back. He could see for a long way down the trail. The pursuit was nowhere in sight.

"Okay, yuh can take it a mite easy now, feller," he told the laboring horse. "Those cayuses back there aren't in yore class. But the black came mighty nigh to being. Plumb sorry I plugged him instead of the sidewinder who was forking him. Hope the hellion busted his neck when he was pitched outa the hull. Mighty pore light for shooting. Didn't seem to bother that jigger over much, though. Another inch to the right and he'd have got me dead center."

He rode silently for some minutes, then remarked aloud:

"Reckon I pulled a plumb loco stunt when I blabbed out there in the Alamita that I figgered to ride to the Bar M and back tonight. Tipped some big-eared gent to the fact that a drygulching was in prime order. If I don't stop underestimating those hellions, I'm gonna end by bustin' up a dull day for the undertaker!"

FIFTEEN

The western section of Alamita was a Mexican quarter, occupied largely by workers in the stamp mills. It was dotted with small *cantinas* and eating houses, where Mexican drinks and dishes were to be had.

Hatfield took to spending considerable time in the quarter, leaning against the *cantina* bars, ordering his drinks always in English, and even at times resorting to signs when he could not otherwise make his desires understood.

Gradually the habitues of the *cantinas* became accustomed to his presence among them and paid him little heed.

One night, as he stood sipping a glass of wine, he heard Jose Muerta's name mentioned by one of two men seated at a nearby table.

"They say *El Presidente's rurales* are out in force," observed the speaker. "They vow to take him without delay."

His table companion laughed scornfully. "The *rurales*!" he jeered. "Let them set their traps in the clouds of the mountaintops, their snares in the morning mists. Let them hope to net the sunbeam glinting on the crest of a ripple, or the little shadow that runs along the ground and loses itself at sunset, but not Jose Muerta!"

"He is a strange man, and able," said the first speaker.

"Aye, a strange man, and one who aims high. His moves are cloaked in mystery and when he strikes, he strikes hard. He is a man of many faces, of strange power. He is here. He is there. He is nowhere. He is seen at a place, and at the same time at another place far distant."

"Nonsense! How can a man be in places more than one at the same time?"

The other glanced about and furtively crossed himself. "There are those," he observed sententiously, "that sell themselves to the Evil One. Perhaps *Don* Jose has paid with the substance of his soul."

"An old wives' tale!" his companion scoffed. "Such stories grow large with the telling. He is but a man of high courage and great daring."

"It is said Governor Bojaco of Sonora has offered the many pesos reward for his head. A great many pesos—a fortune. But none will profit by the offer. *Don* Jose is destined to become great."

"Perhaps, but it will be bad for *Mejico* if he does. He will rule with a hand that will make that of *El Presidente* seem light by comparison. The people will suffer."

"Many pesos reward," the other muttered. "A great fortune. It is said he makes rendezvous on this side of the Great River. If one did but know—"

"Silence! Speak not words that may be wafted none know where. There are ears everywhere. If such words should come to the hearing of—"

The sentence was finished by a significant gesture across the throat. The other man glanced about nervously and relapsed into silence. When the conversation was resumed, it dealt with other matters.

Jim Hatfield left the *cantina* in a very thoughtful frame of mind.

Work on the conveyor line progressed. The towers were built on the relocated sites, the cables strung. Henry Blaine was doing a competent job, Hatfield was forced to admit. No further errors of judgment on his part were apparent.

"Keep the business of the change of engines under yore hat," the Ranger had requested of John Mosby.

"But Blaine will know a change has been made when he sees the engines," Mosby pointed out.

"That'll be soon enough for him to know," Hatfield replied. "I'm just curious to see what he'll say."

"Okay, Jim, if yuh want it that way," Mosby conceded.

But when the engines arrived, Blaine, expertly supervising their installation, made no comment at all.

190

"Looks like the jigger just wrote down the wrong figgers by mistake," Mosby said to Hatfield.

"Uh-huh, it does begin to look that way," the Lone Wolf admitted. "No use to say anything to him about it. No sense in fannin' a feller for a mistake when no harm comes of it."

"Reckon that's right," Mosby admitted.

But to himself, Hatfield said with satisfaction:

"Smart, all right, but a mite too smart. What I figgered might be just a notion of mine now looks to be a straight hunch."

During the days that had passed Hatfield had several times dropped into the Greasy Sack. But each time he had failed to notice John Morton, the new owner, at his accustomed place at the end of the bar. Finally he questioned the head barkeep, a taciturn individual with a truculent eye, as to Morton's whereabouts.

"Off on a trip," the barkeep replied laconically. "Over Arizona way to straighten up some of the loose ends of business he was in over there, I understand. Left here one afternoon a while back, sent word the next morning that he wouldn't be around for a coupla weeks or so. Busy man!"

"Looks that way," Hatfield admitted. "Place 'pears to be runnin' all right without him, though."

The barkeep grunted. "I helped Rose run it for nigh onto five years," he replied. "Yuh sorta get onto the business, whatever it is, when yuh work for Pecos Rose, or yuh don't stay workin' for her. Calc'late I can keep things movin' without help from anybody else. Morton is a smart jigger, though, and I've a notion he won't stand for any foolishness. Quiet, and don't talk much, but he's got a bad eye. Wouldn't wanta buck up against him and wouldn't wanta have a run-in with him. Notion he's got one helluva temper if he ever lets go. That's usu'ly the way with quiet fellers. Liable to see him blow up some day over somethin', and then there'll be fireworks wuth watchin', or I'm a heap mistook."

A couple of days later Hatfield saw the bartender's opinion substantiated.

Visiting the Greasy Sack for a few minutes before riding back to the mine, he found Morton at his accustomed spot at the end of the bar. He was his usual dignified self, immaculate as ever; but Hatfield noted that he moved with a slight stiffness at variance with his former panther-like grace—moved as a man who has recently been doing some long and hard riding. He wondered idly if Morton had made a long trip and back to Arizona via horseback instead of by train.

The Greasy Sack was well crowded, and turbulent. Evidently a number of punchers were in from the neighborhood spreads, doubtless celebrating pay day. They were a good-natured lot, but exuberant with liquor and a holiday spirit. They wrangled amicably over their cards and their drinks, chaffed with the dance floor girls, commented humorously on the quality of the music, comments which were received with good-natured grins by the Mexican musicians.

The floor men and card dealers were watchful and alert, however, as was John Morton. It seemed to Hatfield that Morton was in an exceedingly bad temper. His eyes glinted in the shadow of his low-drawn hatbrim, his jaw was hard set, the bunches of muscle along the dividing line of his cheeks more prominent than usual, his wide nostrils flaring as if he breathed heavily. His attention was chiefly fixed on a nearby table where several poker players appeared to be having a continual argument with the black-coated dealer.

Suddenly the trouble came to a head. One of the cowboys, a brawny, gorilla-armed individual, leaped to his feet with a curse, and slapped the offending dealer clean out of his chair. His companions also came to their feet, plainly ready to back him up.

The floor men rushed forward, but Morton was ahead of them with a catlike bound. The belligerent puncher whirled to meet him and launched a vicious blow at the saloonkeeper's head.

Morton ducked and the other's fist missed his face and merely whisked Morton's hat from his head, not even ruffling a strand of his precisely parted black hair.

Hatfield saw Morton's left hand flash to his head in an instinctive gesture of alarm. Then his right fist lashed out, catching the cowboy in the breast and hurling him backward off balance.

Morton's hand flashed back, his left fingers gripped the lapel of his long black coat, jerking it open. A blur of movement and his hand came from under his left armpit gripping a heavy gun. The black muzzle yawned its deadly menace at the offending cowboy. The hammer came clicking back.

Crash!

Men yelled and ducked at the boom of the report. Morton yelped with pain and reeled back, clutching at his blood spurting fingers. His gun, its stock smashed and shattered, clanged to the floor halfway across the room.

Jim Hatfield, his smoking Colt clamped against his sinewy hip, swept the room with a swift, all-embracing glance which centered on the saloonkeeper. He spoke, his voice quiet, but easily carrying across the room.

"That woulda been mighty like a cold-blooded killing, if yuh'd pulled trigger," he said to Morton. "The other jigger was plumb off balance and hadn't even reached. I've a notion yuh'd have been sorry about now."

Morton stared at him, still gripping his bullet-grazed fingers, his prominent eyes pale and deadly but utterly without expression, his lips drawn back from his gleaming, pointed teeth. Then his face smoothed out, though with visible effort. He essayed a smile, a smile that did not reach his pale eyes and that lifted his lips like the grin of an angry wolf.

"Perhaps you are right," he said in soft, musical tones. "Yes, I believe you are. It would have been a mistake, and I don't often make mistakes. Thank you for saving me that one."

He turned, swept up his hat from the floor and set it carefully on his head. He strode to his fallen gun, picked it up, grimacing at the shattered stock, and holstered it.

Hatfield, after a final glance around the room, slid his own gun back into its sheath. He gestured to the tense group of cowboys. "Get out and sober up," he told them.

The cowboys were already sober, but they obeyed orders without argument, the author of the trouble nodding gratefully to Hatfield as they filed past and out the door. Hatfield turned back to the bar, lifted his brimming glass with a hand that did not spill a drop, and drank it off. The bartender poured another, the bottle neck clicking nervously against the glass rim as he did so.

"Gosh, feller, I'm glad yuh happened to be here," he muttered. "That was touch and go. I told yuh there'd be fireworks if he ever blew up, didn't I? He's a *muy malo hombre!*"

Hatfield was inclined to agree with the drink juggler that John Morton was a "very bad man" when he got started.

"Salty, all right," he mused to himself. "Killer eyes, if ever I saw a pair. And smart enough to know he hasn't any business letting himself go."

He speculated Morton's broad back a moment, downed his drink and left the saloon.

For a long time that night Hatfield sat smoking beside the open window of the darkened bunkhouse, thinking deeply. When he finally went to bed, the concentration furrow was still deep between his black brows, but his stern face wore a pleased expression.

The conveyor line was completed on schedule. Huge iron buckets laden with ore whizzed down the mountainside, rocking and swaying around the turns, rumbling along the taut cable on pulley wheels to dump their contents at the bins of the big new stamp mill John Mosby was erecting in Alamita.

At the Silver City mine, the stamp mill was silent and ready for dismantling. No longer did the great steel pestles do their ponderous dance that crushed the ore to a watery paste from which the precious metal would be extracted by the amalgam process. The frosty balls of quicksilver, charged with their precious load, had been retorted, the quicksilver resolved by roasting to vapor which was chilled by water and once more became valuable mercury. The silver compound, rich also in gold content, had been melted into ponderous bricks which would be conveyed to the Alamita bank and held secure for shipment to the government assay offices.

Before the mine office stood a heavy wagon drawn by six strong draft horses. It waited for its precious load. Lounging in their saddles, armed with rifle and sixgun, were the mine patrol. Jim Hatfield stood a little to one side of the open office door.

From the office filed a line of workmen, bearing the silver bricks. They turned toward the waiting wagon, halted in surprise at the Lone Wolf's abrupt command.

Hatfield gestured to the loading platform of the conveyor system.

"Into the buckets with those bricks, boys," he ordered.

The workers, after momentary hesitation, turned obediently and plodded up the incline to the platform.

Henry Blaine, the mining engineer, who was watching nearby, let out a yelp of astonishment.

"Here, here," he called peremptorily to Hatfield. "Those bricks are to be loaded into this wagon. They're going to Alamita."

"They're going to Alamita, all right, but not by

wagon," the Lone Wolf replied imperturbably. "Sift sand, fellers, yuh're holding up the conveyor line."

"But, listen!" bellowed Blaine. "I'm telling you—"

Hatfield's voice cut through his yammer.

"Blaine, I'm giving the orders here."

"But—but," sputtered Blaine, "I'm the mine engineer. I know—"

"But I'm giving the orders," Hatfield told him with a finality that brooked no further argument.

Blaine subsided, his nervous eyes jumping in his head, muttering under his breath. He glanced uncertainly down the Alamita trail, his gaze shifting to the stable that housed his horse. Hatfield smiled thinly, and said nothing.

Into the big buckets that were lined on the siding cable the bricks were dumped. Finally the tally was complete. Hatfield signaled to the controller on the platform, who jerked the lever and sent the buckets sliding onto the mainline cable. An instant later they were whisking out of sight down the mountainside, flashing past the empty buckets that were ascending via the moving lower cable in a long line.

Hatfield swung into Goldy's saddle. "All right, boys, let's get going," he called to the waiting members of the patrol.

Henry Blaine, biting his nails before the office door, watched the troop vanish swiftly around a turn, a strange gleam in his nervous eyes.

At a hard pace Hatfield led his men down the mountain trail. Paralleling the trail for the most part were the conveyor line cables. The upper cable hummed from the vibration set up by the loaded buckets careening downward. The lower clicked along cheerfully as it drew the empties back to the mine. From time to time thickets or shoulders of rock hid the line from the trail, but always apparent was that deep-toned hum and the sprightly clicking of movement and tension.

Walt Smith chuckled as he rode next to Hatfield's bridle head.

"Jim, that was plumb smart, letting everybody think the bricks were going to town by wagon, with us fellers amblin' along to keep watch over 'em, and then at the last minute, without tellin' anybody, sendin' 'em spinnin' down the mountain in them buckets. If any hellions did have designs on the cleanup, they're thrown plumb off. Mebbe it don't mean anythin', but mebbe it saved us fellers a heap of trouble. There's places along this snake track that're plumb prime for a dry-gulchin', and I wouldn't put anythin' past that sidewinder Muerta."

"I wouldn't, either," Hatfield replied grimly, "and I only hope I played a straight hunch."

"Who all knew about this move?" Smith asked curiously.

"Only John Mosby and myself. We worked

it out together yesterday afternoon," Hatfield replied. "Mosby figgered it was a good notion. Even the control man on the loading platform didn't know why those buckets were being held up."

"Seemed to sorta set Henry Blaine by the ears," chuckled Smith. "I thought for a minute his eyes were gonna jump outa his head."

"Sorta give him a turn for a minute, I reckon," Hatfield agreed. "Reckon he was surprised as anybody else."

"Reckon them bricks are a long ways down the mountain by now, ain't they?" speculated Smith, nearly an hour later.

"They're quite a ways ahead of us," Hatfield agreed. "They—"

"What the blazes!" interrupted Smith.

From somewhere far below sounded a deep rumbling. The patrol members looked questions one to another. They pulled their horses up to listen.

Suddenly Hatfield was aware of something missing. The upper cable still hummed as buckets of ore shot downward; but the steady, rhythmic clicking had ceased. He glanced toward the conveyor line. The upper cable vibrated, but the lower cable hung motionless.

"Sift sand!" he shouted to his men. "Somethin's busted loose down there."

At a mad gallop they raced their horses down

the trail, shooting quick glances to the right, where the conveyor line overhung a long slope that dropped gently to a wide valley floor thickly wooded and spired with crags and chimney rocks. The valley was silent and deserted, void of sound or movement. The slope stretched desolate and lonely.

They covered a mile, part of another. Suddenly from below sounded, thin with distance, the sharp crack of a single rifle shot.

Again the silence descended, broken only by the hum of the upper conveyor cable. Abruptly this ceased also.

"They know something is wrong up at the mine; they've stopped sending down buckets," Hatfield said. "Sift sand, yuh jugheads!"

Goldy could have easily outstripped the other horses, but Hatfield felt that it was wise to keep the troop together. He restrained the sorrel, governing his speed to that of the slowest horse.

They flashed past the site of one of the relay engines. Nobody was in sight.

"Feller hustled down to see what happened," Hatfield deduced. "Pore devil, I've a notion what he learned didn't do him any good," he added, thinking of that single ominous rifle shot.

Another half-mile of furious riding. They rounded a shoulder of rock, swept past a thicket that for some hundreds of yards hid the conveyor line, and a scene of wreckage and disaster met their eyes.

One of the tall towers lay in splintered ruin on the ground. Empty buckets, and others spilling ore, lay scattered about in wild confusion. Both cables were snapped off short and lay trailing amid the brush. Crawling painfully toward the trail was a man who dragged one helpless leg behind him as he inched forward on his hands and one knee. Hatfield recognized the engineer of the relay engine they had just passed.

SIXTEEN

Hatfield sent Goldy charging down the slope to the conveyor line. He swung to the ground as the sorrel skittered to a halt, and knelt beside the injured man.

"What happened, feller?" he asked anxiously.

"Half a dozen men, mebbe more," panted the engineer. "They was loadin' the bricks inter pack sacks on horses. I heard the blast and hustled down here to see what was goin' on. They musta blowed the tower with dynamite. They shot me in the leg—knocked me down the slope inter the brush. Reckon they calc'lated they'd done me in—didn't come down to finish me."

"Where'd they go?" Hatfield asked.

The engineer motioned vaguely toward the valley floor. "Down there somewhere," he replied. "I couldn't see over good through the brush, and I was purty sick."

Hatfield nodded grimly. He deftly cut away the britches leg and got a tourniquet around the injured limb to stanch the bleeding. He roughly bandaged the wounded member with handkerchiefs and strips torn from his shirt.

"Just a clean hole through the flesh," he told the engineer. "No bones busted; yuh'll be okay in a few weeks." Then he stood up and stared into the valley, shaking his head.

There was no means of telling which way the outlaws might have gone, in that silent, pathless expanse of bush. He stood thinking furiously. Suddenly his eyes glowed with inspiration.

"Crane," he told one of the patrolmen, "you stay here and look after this feller. The rest of yuh come with me."

Mounting, he sent Goldy racing back up the trail, the others thundering behind.

"I'm playing a hunch I know where the hellions are heading for," he told his men. "The chances are they'll know a side canyon that will lead them outa that valley. They'll be following the chord of the arc—the short way. We'll be going around the curve—the long way. But those pack horses will be carrying heavy loads and should slow them down. Mebbe we can catch them up before they get in the clear. It's a chance, anyhow, and I figger it's wuth taking."

"But how in blazes did they know the bricks were coming down the conveyor line?" Smith demanded. "Yuh didn't even tell us fellers about it."

This question Hatfield did not attempt to answer—yet.

A mile below the mine site, they met a buckboard loaded with repair men seeking the cause of the conveyor line breaking down.

"Just below Number Five relay engine," Hatfield roared to them without slacking speed. He sent Goldy foaming up the last steep stretch that led to the mine.

They flashed past the mine site, heedless of the shouts and questions volleyed at them, and thundered westward along the Tornillo Trail. Hatfield did not slacken speed until he reached the point where the dim side track branched from the Tornillo. Here he pulled up, narrowly scanning the brush that fringed the track. He rode along it a little way, and with an exclamation of satisfaction pointed out the numerous broken and dangling twigs that scarred the growth.

"The packs brushing against the chaparral did that," he explained. "Fellers, we're on the right track, or I'm a heap mistook. Easy, now, and keep yore eyes and ears open. It's a salty outfit we're after, and if they hear us coming and get the drop on us, it'll be curtains."

The patrol pushed forward with as much speed as they dared. They could see but a short distance in front at all times; more often their range of vision was limited to a few yards. They listened intently, but no sound broke the stillness of the mountainside.

They reached the long slope below which had occurred the wreck of the Sunset Flyer, but still no sign of the owlhoots. Hatfield began to wonder uneasily if after all his hunch was wrong. His jaw set grimly at the thought.

Another mile, two, and still the trail wound

silent and deserted, veering steadily to the south, having crossed the railroad tracks some distance back.

Suddenly Hatfield held up his hand. His companions, straining their ears, caught the sound of a faint rustling, as if a heavy object was being dragged through the brush somewhere ahead.

"It's the pack saddles brushing against the growth," Hatfield said in low tones. "All set, now. We'll be on top of them any minute. Fast work, and shoot straight."

The trail swept around a shoulder of rock, straightened out, widened somewhat and curved again.

Mouth grimly set, eyes pale flames in his bleak face, Hatfield sent Goldy racing forward. They hurtled around the bend, the trail straightened out and widened once more; and less than a hundred yards in front of them was the owlhoot band, riding bunched together, flogging the laboring pack horses.

They whirled in their saddles as the patrol thundered around the bend. A crashing volley met them, and a hail of hissing lead.

The owlhoots tried to fight back, tried with the desperation of cornered rats, but they were caught totally unprepared. Saddles were emptied at that first volley. The terrified pack animals reared and plunged in hopeless confusion, adding to the panic. Again the roar of the patrol guns and again men went down. Others fired wildly, hardly taking time to aim.

A patrolman yelped a curse as a chance bullet cut the flesh of his arm. Another reeled in the saddle, blood spurting from his creased shoulder. Hatfield's guns roared a drumroll of fire. And abruptly ahead were only wildly flying riderless horses crashing through the brush, and the maddened tangle of the plunging pack animals.

Out of the whirling mass shot a great black horse. Hatfield caught a glimpse of a tall figure bending low in the saddle. The sunlight glimmered for an instant on hair the color of burnished gold. Then horse and rider vanished around a bend in the trail.

"Stay here with the stuff, and see if any of the sidewinders are still alive!" Hatfield shouted to his men. His voice rang out like the clang of a great bronze bell:

"Trail, Goldy! Trail!"

The sorrel shot forward and an instant later was entangled in the milling stampede of the pack horses.

It took Hatfield minutes to break through the mess. And when he rounded the bend in the trail, the fugitive was nowhere in sight.

"And that cayuse he was forkin' is a wonder, or I miss my bet," he growled disgustedly. "Is that yaller-haired hellion allus going to get the breaks! Sift sand, jughead, yuh got more work cut out for yuh this time, or I'm a heap mistook."

Goldy responded with everything that was in him. Hatfield, crouching low in the saddle, his right hand hovering over the black butt of his gun, scanned the trail ahead, the brush on either side. But there was no sight of the golden-haired man on the black horse.

They covered a mile, and a second. Hatfield glanced frowningly at the sky. The lower edge of the sun was almost touching the western crags.

"Once it gets dark, I might as well try to rope a flea on a sheep's back!" he growled disgustedly.

The sun sank lower. Shadows were drifting down the slopes. The trail, flanked for the most part by tall brush, was already growing gloomy. Hatfield peered ahead with greater intentness. They rounded a curve, Goldy leaning far over to keep his balance. Hatfield surged erect, his voice rang out:

"Up, Goldy! Up!"

The sorrel did his best, bounding high into the air as if on springs; but try as he would, one front leg slammed against the taut rope stretched waist high across the trail.

Goldy shot through the air as if he had taken unto himself wings. Hatfield barely had time to free his feet from the stirrups and hurl himself sideways before the sorrel hit the ground with a bone-breaking thud. His rider was hurtled far to one side to crash through the thick growth and likewise thud to the ground.

From the growth a few yards down the trail spurted reddish flame. A bullet fanned Hatfield's face. Three times the hidden drygulcher fired, clipping twigs from the bushes and showering the Ranger's prostrate form with splinters. But Hatfield had landed in a slight depression and the whining slugs missed him by a hair. Through the mist of his whirling senses, he dimly heard the click of fast hoofs fading quickly into the distance.

SEVENTEEN

For minutes Hatfield lay stunned by the shock. Gradually his head cleared and he essayed to sit up. Thankfully he found that there was no limb that would not move, no joint that would not bend. He managed to scuffle erect and stood swaying dizzily.

His first thought was for his horse. With heartfelt relief, he found Goldy on his feet, with skinned knees and a patch knocked off one shoulder. He limped slightly as he moved toward the Ranger with a plaintive whinny, but was evidently not badly injured.

After giving his mount a careful once-over, Hatfield climbed stiffly into the saddle and turned Goldy's head back up-trail. Sadly mauled and battered, he made his way back to where he had left his men. He was seething with anger—anger not altogether directed at the man who had worsted him.

" 'Pears every time I take a trick from that hellion, he comes right back and trumps my ace!" he growled disgustedly. In fact, he was beginning to feel that never in his Ranger career had he had such an opponent as Jose Muerta.

"Or is it Muerta I'm really up against?" he muttered morosely. "I'm sure beginning to wonder." A little later he added grimly:

210

"But about next time I'm going to play the joker!"

Hatfield found the patrolmen waiting where he had left them. They had lighted a fire and were squatting around it, alert and watchful. They had laid out the dead owlhoots in an orderly row.

"Six of the hellions all cashed in proper," Walt Smith told Hatfield, after they had relieved their concern over his various cuts and scratches and bruises. "None of 'em lived long enough to do any talkin', wuss luck. Four 'pear to be out-and-out Yaqui Injuns, but the other two are white—Texans, I'd say, ornery lookin' side-winders. Nothin' in their pockets, of co'hse, and the horses they were forkin' wear some crazy Mexican brand that don't mean nothin'."

" 'Bout as would be expected," Hatfield agreed. He carefully examined the bodies, but discovered nothing overlooked by the men.

"Well, reckon we might as well pack this dinero back to the mine," he decided. "We'll run it to town tomorrow. Reckon they won't make another try just yet."

"Not likely, the way we're whittlin' the gang down," Smith said.

"But the head of the snake is still floppin' around loose," Hatfield pointed out. "Give it a mite of time and it'll grow a new body. We've gotta squash the head if we ever expect to have any peace."

John Mosby was at the mine when they arrived there, long after midnight. He voiced profane relief at the recovery of the stolen cleanup.

"Anybody hurt bad?" he inquired.

"Oh, Curly's got a hunk of meat knocked outa his shoulder, and Blount has a furrow in his left arm. Goldy and me have lost considerable hide but there's nothing to lose sleep over," Hatfield replied. He turned to ask a question of Walt Smith, but the latter was nowhere to be seen.

"Come inter the office, John," he requested the mine owner. "I want a word with you."

When they were inside the office, with the door shut, Hatfield asked a question:

"John, did yuh tell anybody about that scheme of ours to run the bricks to town by way of the conveyor line?"

"Why, no, that is nobody except Lynn Dawson and Henry Blaine," Mosby replied. "We had chuck t'gether in the Anytime last night and I discussed it with them. They both figgered it was a swell notion. Yuh don't figger, Jim—"

"I figger somebody sure talked outa turn," Hatfield cut in.

"Mebbe some dog-eared hellion overheard us talkin' at the table," hazarded Mosby.

"Could be," Hatfield admitted noncommittally. "Anyhow, *Don* Jose and his hellions got wind of it, and mighty nigh got away with it, too."

"Thanks to you, they didn't," Mosby returned.

"I won't forget this day's work soon, Jim."

Hatfield nodded but did not reply. He was thinking of Henry Blaine's actions when the shipment was diverted from the wagon apparently intended for it to the conveyor line. His black brows drew together.

"Mebbe just an act for the benefit of anybody who might be hanging around," he mused. "Sorta on a par with him not saying a word about the changed horsepower of the relay engines. He put on a good act that time, too."

He debated questioning the mine engineer, but decided against it. Blaine would undoubtedly have a plausible explanation for feigning ignorance of the change in plans relative to the shipment.

The bricks were taken to Alamita the following day, convoyed by the entire guard force. The trip was made without mishap and the metal stored in the bank vault to await shipment to the assay office.

Hatfield dropped into the Greasy Sack for a drink, after disposing of his charge. John Morton was not present, but Lynn Dawson sat at a corner table, sipping a drink. Of late, Dawson had been seen more often in the Greasy Sack than in the Anytime. He spent most of his time at the bank, varied with occasional trips to the Silver City. He also took an active part in superintending the construction of the new stamp mill.

Dawson was hatless, the rays of an overhanging lamp striking full on his light brown hair, which was inclined to wave. As Hatfield passed the table, he glanced down at the bank manager's bared head. He hesitated in his stride, almost halted, then passed on, his brows drawing together. Dawson, peering through his tinted lenses, was apparently oblivious of his presence.

Several days later news came to Alamita of Jose Muerta's exploits below the line. His mountain fighters, abetted by the *peons* who hailed him as *El Libertador*, had routed a strong force of *rurales* sent against them by *El Presidente*.

"Them black hellions cut up the wounded, crucified them on cactus spines, spread-eagled 'em over ant hills," said the man who brought the word. "Nice folks! They say the Rangers are patrolling the border, and that *El Presidente* is sending troops inter Chihuahua from Mexico City."

"Helluva lot of good they'll do," grunted John Mosby. "Muerta will just play hide-and-go-seek with 'em through the hills till he gets 'em where he wants 'em, then he'll mow 'em down. It's a hell's pity somebody don't mow him down. With him done in, the whole thing would fold up overnight."

"They say the bullet ain't run what can down him," a cowboy remarked. "Sure is beginnin' to look that way. He just comes and goes as he pleases. Never can tell where he's gonna show up next. Why, he might be right here in town right now, lookin' over yore shoulder."

A nervous twisting of heads greeted the remark. The puncher chuckled. His hearers grinned and looked foolish.

"Just the same, that don't come as nigh to bein' a joke as it might," one of them commented. "Before now he's raided this side the river when he was s'posed to be a hundred miles off. I tell yuh, the hellion ain't human!"

There was a general nodding of heads.

"Salty Craig Wilson ain't showed up no great shakes agin him," the cowboy who had first spoken remarked. "Reckon this is about the fust time Craig ever hadda eat dust. I've a notion he don't over like the taste of it, either."

"Craig'll drop a loop on the sidewinder yet, see if he don't," John Mosby squeaked. "I'm gonna suggest he makes that big feller Hatfield a dep'ty and let him turn loose his wolf on Muerta. He's come mighty nigh to downin' him a coupla times already. I've a hunch Muerta wouldn't be over anxious to tangle with him."

"A salty jigger, all right," the cowboy agreed, "but Muerta! Well—"

"By the way," Lynn Dawson said in his musical voice, "just who is Hatfield, and where did he come from? Does anybody know?"

A silence followed. "Why, I never figgered to

ask him," said John Mosby. "Never was much on askin' a feller questions so long as he 'peared to be on the up-and-up."

"And that fellow Smith—the one with the whiskers—does anybody know anything about him?" Dawson persisted. "All of a sudden he happened along in Hatfield's company."

"What yuh tryin' to get at anyhow, Lynn?" Mosby demanded.

Dawson peered up at him in his near-sighted way.

"Oh, nothing," he disclaimed, "only things sure have been happening since that pair landed here."

Old John snorted derisively, but the others looked meditative.

"Yuh don't mean to intimate that there's somethin' off-color about Hatfield and Smith, do yuh?" demanded old John. "Why, they tangled Muerta's rope twice for him, and Hatfield mighty nigh busted up that robbery at the mine that night."

"But whoever it was held up the mine did get away with it, after all, didn't they?" Dawson pointed out. "And what proof do you have that Muerta had anything to do with those jobs? Who saw Muerta to recognize him? Who maintained it was Muerta? Only Hatfield and Smith. I'm not saying they didn't prevent the train robbery, or that one of the conveyor system; but perhaps they had reasons of their own, who can tell? Outlaws have been known to fall out among themselves before now."

"Bosh!" Mosby exploded, but just the same his brow knotted querulously.

Walt Smith had been visiting the Fiddle-Back spread whenever he got the chance.

"Keeps me busy gettin' there fust ahead of that Dawson jigger," he confided to Hatfield one afternoon, after returning from one of his trips to Pecos Rose's ranch house. "I figger Helen feels sorta sorry for him because of his eyes. Inc'dentally, he told Helen the other day that he's figgerin' on bein' away for a spell. Says he's goin' over East to have his eyes op'rated on. Says that if he has the op'ration, he'll be able to see nigh as well as anybody, afterward. Wonder if that's so?"

"Could be," Hatfield admitted noncommittally. "Doctors can do some unusual things nowadays. Many a man whose vision has been impaired by an injury or a sickness has had it restored by the proper operation or treatment. Might be the case with Dawson. Looks like he must have something definite to base the statement on."

His brows drew together in thought as he spoke, and he was unusually silent the remainder of the evening.

Another man who seemed to be making numerous trips somewhere or other was John

Morton. In fact, he seemed to be more out of his new property than in it, leaving the running of the saloon to the efficient head bartender.

"But he drops in when yuh least expect him," the barkeep confided to Hatfield. "Any hour of the day or night. He was gone five days last week, then all of a sudden here he was just about closin' time. Sorta keeps the boys on their toes, all right. They never know but what they'll turn around any time and find him lookin' over their shoulders. He's a hard one to figger, but he's a good man to work for. Raised everybody's pay already, and all he asks is that a feller be on the job. Insists that the games be run plumb straight, and that the right stuff is in the bottle yuh pour. He says Pecos Rose made it pay that way and don't figger why he should change.

"'Make a little quick money, and end up by losin' a good customer,' is the way he says it. He's right, too. A square dealin' jigger allus comes out on top, sooner or later. The other kind allus ends up in the cactus patch."

"Yuh got something there, feller," Hatfield agreed. "Mebbe it takes time, but in the end that's the way it works out."

Smith got the afternoon off a few days later and rode to the Fiddle-Back. Pecos Rose met him at the door of the ranch house with a pleasant smile. The look she bent upon the tall young fellow was distinctly approving. A little later, he and Helen went off together for a ride.

It was a soft gray day and very lovely. The first frost of early autumn had passed lightly over the hilltops the night before and the forests were splashed with scarlet and with gold. A mellow haze drifted down from the hills and there was a hush in the air that was crisply cold. Overhead the clouds massed heavily, wreathing into fantastic shapes before a wind that was not felt on the ground below. The prairie grasses were touched with amethyst and pale amber, and bronzed along the stream edges and in low places by the fading ferns. Stately purple asters nodded on the banks of the brooks and their reflections made asters in the brooks.

The clouds thickened and seemed to drift lower. A gloom as of approaching evening shrouded the land and, where the growth was tall, the shadows were dark.

Walt Smith and Helen Marcy rode mostly in silence. There seemed to be little need of words between them. Only the girl's soft color came and went entrancingly as the gaze of the man by her side rested upon her. Seemingly they rode alone; but in reality there was another, unseen, unheard, who rode with them and smiled upon their vigor and freshness with approving eyes, that king of kings, who with a wave of the heart-shaped bow that is his scepter levels barriers of face and faith and conditions. That old, old tyrant who will brook no rival in the kingdom of youth.

"Looks like it might storm," Smith observed at length. "Reckon we'd better be turnin' back, don't you?"

Helen nodded without words, her eyes on the far blue hills to the west, where the crags fanged up against the sky, behind them the pale glow of the cloud-veiled setting sun.

To their left was the rolling vastness of the rangeland. To their right, less than a hundred yards distant, a dark bristle of growth shrouded with shadows, seeming to crouch like some waiting monster in the fading light.

Walt Smith leaned over impulsively and reached for the girl's hand. His movement was unexpectedly abrupt, a quick swaying of his lithe form in the saddle.

And at that instant reddish fire spurted from the dark fringe of growth. The stillness was shattered to shreds by a crashing report. Helen Marcy screamed chokingly as Walt Smith reeled back, slumped from the saddle and lay prone on the ground, his bloody face buried in the amber grasses.

EIGHTEEN

One of the mine patrol brought the news of the shooting of Walt Smith to the Silver City.

"He was hit purty bad," the informant told Jim Hatfield. "Deep gash cut in his head. Doc said if the slug had been a quarter of an inch to the left we woulda had a buryin'. The town's all het up about it. Ord'nary drygulchin's are bad enough, but plugging a jigger when he's out ridin' with a gal is goin' a mite too far. Why, at that time of the evenin' it was gettin' so dark a feller could hardly see to line sights. He coulda just as easy shot the gal. A hell's wonder he didn't! Stretchin' rope is too good for that sidewinder, whoever he is. Craig Wilson rode out to the Fiddle-Back this mawnin', but didn't learn nothin' what would do any good. Smith says he ain't no idea who'd want to do him in. John Mosby has offered a big reward for the horned toad, and I understand the county commissioners are calc'latin' to double it.

"Funny thing Lynn Dawson said," the mine guard added. "We was talkin' about the shootin' this afternoon in the Anytime. Mosby was there, and Dawson, and Henry Blaine. All of a sudden Dawson squinted up at Mosby through his glasses. 'Rec'lect what I told yuh the other evenin', John?' he said."

"What did Mosby say?" Hatfield asked quietly.

"John didn't say nothin'. He just cussed, and looked worried."

Half an hour later, Hatfield was riding swiftly to Alamita.

It was past banking hours when he arrived in town, but he found John Mosby in his office at the bank, conferring with Lynn Dawson and Henry Blaine, the mining engineer.

"John," he told the banker, when he was admitted to the office, "I want yuh to ride to the Fiddle-Back with me, right away."

Mosby hesitated, glancing at the papers littering his desk. "All right," he agreed reluctantly. "Reckon this business can wait. I'll take it up with yuh again tomorrow, Lynn," he concluded, gathering the papers together and rising to his feet.

Dawson and Blaine exchanged swift glances which were not lost on Hatfield. The Ranger smiled thinly, but made no comment.

"I'm gettin' sorta pressed for ready money," Mosby confided to Hatfield as they rode north by east across the darkening prairie. "Lynn knows some folks over East and figgers we can get the money from them by givin' mortgages on the Silver City. It's about the only thing I got left that isn't already tied up to the hilt. After the new stamp mill gets goin' good, I'll be settin' purty, but right now it's got me scratchin'."

Hatfield nodded. "I've a notion things will clear up soon," he comforted.

"That dad-burned row below the line is havin' its effect," Mosby said wrathfully. "Folks are gettin' worried and money's tight. Investors are sorta chary about puttin' out dinero to finance projects in a section where what might happen is uncertain. Yuh were right, Jim, already I'm seein' that what that hellion does down there has its effect on us up here."

They rode on mostly in silence with only a word now and then relative to unimportant matters until they reached the Fiddle-Back.

Pecos Rose admitted them to the ranch house and led them to a bedroom where Walt Smith lay propped up with pillows. Helen Marcy hovered about the bed and Smith, pale of face and haggard, nevertheless had a decidedly contented look in his eyes. His face lighted with pleasure when the form of the Lone Wolf towered in the doorway; but the look was replaced with one of consternation when he saw John Mosby's bulk beside him.

Hatfield smiled, a sunny look in his green eyes. He walked to the bed and took Smith's hand.

"Walt," he said, "seeing as yuh came mighty nigh to taking the big jump and are sorta knocked out for a spell, I figgered I'd oughta bring yore dad in to have a look at yuh."

Helen Marcy looked up wide-eyed. Pecos Rose

smiled, as if the startling statement did not tell her anything she didn't already know. Walt Smith stared with a hanging jaw. Old John Mosby gulped and goggled like a newly landed fish.

Chuckling under his breath, Hatfield drew Mosby to the bed. Old John stared down at the pale, bearded face on the pillow.

"Why—why, Wade!" he stuttered. "Why—son, I wouldn't have knowed yuh, with all that brush on yore face!"

The man on the bed grinned up wanly. "Yuh—yuh see, Dad," he hesitated, "I had an awful hankerin' to see yuh again, but I didn't want yuh to know me—comin' back busted and out of a job, as yuh allus said I would."

"To hell with that!" exploded old John. "I'm almighty glad to see yuh in any shape, almighty glad!"

His son chuckled, his bearded lips quirking wryly. "Rec'lect, Dad, what we had the row about when I pulled out? It was over you wantin' me to go to work for yuh. Well, looks like yuh won out after all. Yuh see, I am workin' for yuh!

"And if it's agreeable with you," he added, "I'm plumb willin' to keep on workin' for yuh, doin' anythin' yuh want me to do."

Old John gripped his son's hand. Pecos Rose chuckled. Helen gazed happily on the scene through a mist of tears.

A moment later, Mosby turned to speak to

Hatfield; but the Lone Wolf, deciding that his presence was become wholly unnecessary, had quietly slipped from the room.

West by south the Ranger rode, his face set in bleak lines, his eyes coldly gray. Instinctively he loosened the heavy guns in the holsters tapping against his thighs. As he reached the outskirts of Alamita, he fumbled something from a cunningly concealed pocket in his broad leather belt.

Hatfield hesitated a moment in front of the Anytime. Then he tethered Goldy at the hitchrack across the street, glanced once through the plate glass window and walked purposefully down Chuckawalla Street.

The Greasy Sack was well crowded despite the lateness of the hour. The poker tables were filled. The roulette wheels whirled, the faro bank was busy. Men lined the bar, and hands reached over the shoulders of the favored who could get a foot on the brass rail. The sprightly click of high heels vied with the solider clump of miner and cowboy boots on the dance floor. The orchestra appeared well oiled and played vigorously. The overhead swinging lamps sent a soft glow over the room that failed to altogether disperse the shadows in the corners.

At the far end of the long bar, John Morton stood conversing earnestly in low tones with Lynn Dawson and Henry Blaine, the Silver City mining engineer. There was a tenseness about Morton that was not usually apparent, and he kept shooting glances under his hatbrim toward the swinging doors. Blaine also seemed nervous and ill at ease. Dawson, on the contrary, was his usual contained self, immaculately garbed, his eyes glinting behind the dark lenses of his glasses. He held a brimming glass in his hand as he spoke, and not a drop of the liquor spilled over the rim.

Suddenly a hush fell on the big room. Morton turned quickly to glance toward the swinging doors. He stiffened, staring with outthrust neck. Dawson quietly set his glass on the bar and seemed to follow Morton's gaze with his shielded eyes. Henry Blaine gulped chokingly in his throat.

The doors had swung open, and just inside stood Jim Hatfield. His face was set in bleak lines. His steady eyes, which were fixed on the tense group at the far end of the bar, were cold as the wind-driven raindrops that were spatting the window panes. On his broad breast gleamed *a silver star set on a silver circle,* the feared and honored badge of the Texas Rangers!

Hatfield took two long strides down the room and paused, erect and towering, thumbs hooked over his double cartridge belts. His voice rang out, vibrant with authority, edged with steel:

"Jose Muerta, I arrest you for robbery and

murder! And that goes for you, too, Lynn Dawson!"

The quivering silence that followed was shattered by Henry Blaine's high-pitched scream.

"I told you he was a Ranger! *I told you he was the Lone Wolf!* You wouldn't listen!"

As if the frenzied shriek had touched a hidden trigger, John Morton ripped a Spanish curse from between his writhing lips and moved with the speed of a striking snake. His right hand shot across his breast to the shoulder gun under his left arm.

Hatfield drew and shot him, before Morton could clear leather. At the same instant he hurled himself sideways. He had seen the lightning forward flicker of Lynn Dawson's hand.

A heavy double-barreled derringer spatted into Dawson's palm and belched fire. The room rocked to the booming report.

A lock of black hair spun from Hatfield's head. He reeled slightly from the shock of the bullet that grazed his skull. Then he fired twice, the reports merging in a single thunder of sound.

Dawson staggered back as if shoved by a mighty hand. He crashed into a table, taking it to the floor with him in splintered ruin.

Henry Blaine was diving wildly for the door. Hatfield leaped forward and caught him a slashing blow alongside the head with the barrel of his Colt. Then, without a second glance at the senseless, bleeding form of the engineer, he walked forward and gazed down at the two dead men on the floor at the end of the bar. He shot one swift, all embracing glance around the room. There was no sign of further hostilities. Men were staring in awe at the almost legendary figure of the Lone Wolf, whose exploits were the talk of Texas, of the whole Southwest.

Hatfield holstered his gun and squatted beside Morton. With a quick move of his hand, he wrenched a black wig from Morton's head, revealing hair that gleamed yellow in the lamplight. He plucked the precise mustache from his upper lip. From the dead man's nostrils he drew hollow quills. Forcing the clenched teeth apart, he dug wads of gum from the spaces between the cheeks and the jawbone.

Morton's wide nostrils drew together. His cheeks, so broad at the base, sank in. The contours of his face subtly changed.

Men crowding behind the Ranger stared down at the lean, high-nosed countenance.

"Blazes!" a voice bellowed. "It *is* Muerta! Well, I'll be damned!"

"And what about the other one?" somebody demanded. "What about Dawson? How could he see to shoot like that?"

Dawson's glasses had fallen from his staring eyes. Hatfield picked them up, held them for the crowd to see.

"Just tinted window glass," he said, with a mirthless laugh. "In this light he could see as good as anybody. Just as he could see as good as anybody the gray, cloudy afternoon when he plugged Walt Smith."

"Here comes the sheriff!" a voice bawled above the babble of comment.

Sheriff Craig Wilson hurried into the room, Skeeter Ellis close at his heels. He cast a swift glance at the star on Hatfield's breast, nodded with little apparent surprise.

"Had oughta knowed it fust off," he said. "Yuh got the looks of a Ranger, and yuh shore act like one. So yuh got Muerta at last, eh? Well, I reckon that busts up the rev'lution the other side the river. Uh-huh, one rev'lution, one Ranger. Reckon that makes the odds about even."

NINETEEN

The following afternoon, Hatfield talked with Sheriff Wilson and John Mosby in the living room of the Fiddle-Back ranch house. Wade Mosby, who had been Walt Smith, was propped up on a couch. Helen Marcy sat beside him, holding his hand. Pecos Rose, a distinctly pleased look on her face, was also present, as were several prominent citizens of Alamita and the surrounding rangeland.

"Henry Blaine talked when he got his senses back," Sheriff Wilson observed. "He tied up the loose ends for us and told us where to glom onto the rest of the outfit up here. We grabbed four at the Silver City mine, and a couple more in town. I reckon that about cleans up the sidewinders on this side the line. *El Presidente* and his *rurales* will take care of what's left down below."

Hatfield nodded. "Blaine was just a sort of hired man stringing along with Dawson," he said. "Dawson took him inter camp. Dawson kinda made a mistake there. Blaine was a weak sort and didn't have much nerve. Dawson, of co'hse, was the real force behind the hull business."

"I still can't see how yuh managed to figger things out like yuh did," commented Sheriff Wilson.

"Dawson really tipped himself off when he took that shot at Wade Mosby," Hatfield replied. "He was the only jigger I could figger out who had any real reason for wanting to do Wade in. Wade didn't appear to be of any importance hereabouts. He was just one of the mine guards, as Walt Smith. Why should anybody go to all the trouble to drygulch him like that? The Muerta gang, because of what he did that day at the train wreck? Didn't look reasonable. Hellions of that sort don't go around taking big chances where there's nothing to be gained. Dawson had a reason for wanting Wade out of the way. He saw Wade was getting the inside track with Helen Marcy, and he wanted her for himself. Then, too, though I'm not sure about it, he might have tumbled to the fact, as I did, that Walt Smith was really John Mosby's son, and figgered he might make trouble for Dawson when he was all set to pull the props from under John and get control of the Silver City mine as he planned to do. I figger the folks over East who were ready to lend yuh money and take mortgages on the mine for security, John, were either some of Dawson's gang or didn't really exist at all. If Dawson had managed to make it impossible for you to meet yore notes, it would have ended up with Dawson owning the notes, of that I'm sure. He knew, of co'hse, that the Silver City is wuth a fortune once it gets going good, and wanted to get hold of it, though that was just one of the irons he had in the fire, a small one.

"But to get back to the shooting. That gray, almost dark day was perfect for the kind of eyes Dawson had, and convinced me it was Dawson drygulched Wade. I was ready to take a chance on throwing down on him after that."

"What kind of eyes did he have?" interpolated old John. "I allus figgered he was blind as a bat."

"He wasn't anything like as blind as he led folks to believe, although on a bright, sunny day, or in a real bright light, I've a notion he could hardly see at all," Hatfield replied. "On a dark, gray day or in dim moonlight he could see as good as anybody. In fact, under such conditions, he could see as well as the average person could in a real bright light. Dawson came mighty nigh to being a hemeralopic."

"What in blazes is that?" demanded Mosby.

"Hemeralopia," Hatfield explained, "is a condition of the eyes in which a jigger can *see clearly* only at night, in a faint light, or on a very dull, dark day. An owl is a nacherel hemeralopic. At night he can see fine, but in the daytime he's practically blind. Some folks are born that way, but the condition is sometimes caused by injury to the eyes or the optic nerve, such as might come about by a piece of the skull bone pressing lightly on a certain portion of the brain. That, I figger, was Dawson's case. One night in the saloon, I got a good look at his head when he had his hat off. The light from a swinging lamp was shining right down on him, and it showed a deep dent in his head just above the hairline over the left temple. The chances are it was an old injury that caused his condition. I figger Dawson, who had owlhoot tendencies, realized, after he was hurt, how he could play up his peculiar condition to his own advantage, putting on a act of being mighty nigh blind, and then cashing in on his ability to see so well at night."

"Then when he told me he was going East to have an operation performed on his eyes, he really meant it!" exclaimed Helen.

"Mebbe," Hatfield admitted, "but more likely he was figgering a trip down Mexico way to look after the ruckus he'd started down there and planned to come back and pretend he'd had an operation. All he'd need to do was stop putting on his blind act. He still wouldn't hafta let anybody know how he could see at night. Reckon he figgered he'd sorta have a better chance with you, then. Funny things a jigger will do when he gets interested in a girl."

His glance rested on Wade Mosby for an instant, and Helen blushed at the smile in his eyes.

"I got my fust notion about Dawson's eyes the night Wade fust saw Helen in the Greasy Sack," Hatfield resumed. "She got flustered when Wade looked at her, and Dawson noticed it. He forgot himself and did something that a really blind man would never do. He turned around and looked straight at Wade. I caught the glint of his eyes behind his glasses and knew he was really seeing what he looked at. That got me to thinking about some things that had struck me at the time they happened as sorta queer.

"There was the night of the mine robbery, the night I fust landed in this section. The feller who shot at me, and missed me by about an inch, when it was so dark I couldn't see him—when the moon broke through the clouds, he threw up his hand to shield his eyes from the light. I thought at the time he was just aiming to hide his face. Then, when he tied me and Welch in that shack, he put out the lamp and walked around just like it was daylight. Then again the jigger that headed the bunch who tried to run me down on the trail from the Bar M to town—he did some almighty fancy shooting in the dark. All that tied up with what I was beginning to think about Dawson's eyes."

"Did yuh think that Dawson might be Muerta?" Wilson asked.

"At fust it had me wondering, although it didn't really seem probable," Hatfield admitted. "They were about the same height and gen'ral build, and in a pore light, Dawson's hair showed about the same color as Muerta's. He cashed in on the resemblance, all right. But when I trailed the jigger I was sure was Muerta the day they robbed the conveyor line, I knew it wasn't Dawson. That jigger cut down on me when I was lying on the ground, but he shot just like a jigger would shoot who couldn't see well in a dim light. If that had been Dawson, I wouldn't be here telling yuh about it. He would have seen me lying under the brush and woulda drilled me dead center. By that time, too, I was beginning to figger Morton as Muerta."

"What did yuh base it on, Jim?" asked Mosby.

"Well, for one thing, Morton was allus away at times when we figgered Muerta was pulling something. For instance, after I had that run-in on the trail from the Bar M, I knocked over the horse the feller I figgered to be Muerta was riding, and gave the rider a mighty hard fall. Right after that, Morton dropped outa sight a coupla weeks. Reckon he was getting over the effects of having been pitched outa the hull that night. When he showed up in the Greasy Sack again, he moved around stiff like, as if he might have recently been stove up somehow. Then that night he had a run-in with those Lazy U cowhands. He got his hat knocked off and I got a good look at his hair and eyes. The hair didn't look at all right to me. The part in it was a mite too precise, and the hair stayed in place as if it was glued. And when his hat went off Morton's

235

fust thought was for his hair; he reached up and felt of it, which was a funny thing for a jigger to do when he was in the middle of a fust class wring. Then his eyes—they were the kinda eyes I'd heard folks say Muerta had, the kind of eyes yuh don't often see. I figgered that night Morton wore a wig. Why should he wear one? Of co'hse fellers without much hair sometimes wear 'em. But I gave his mustache a close once-over and it didn't look right either. Things were beginning to tie up. There was something else, too.

"The night before the Sanders bank was robbed, months back, I was riding the Tornillo Trail to Franklin and Ranger headquarters. That night I met Muerta and his bunch at a fork of the trail. When he saw me, by a lightning flash, Muerta turned his men to the right. He shouted out an order, and he made a gesture with his hand. Well, one night in the Greasy Sack, Morton steered a waiter who was making a mistake to the right. He barked out an order and used his hand just like Muerta had that fust time I saw him. I noticed it right off, but at the time I didn't tie it up with Muerta, of co'hse; that came later when I got to wondering more about Morton."

"Ain't anythin' much yuh don't notice," grunted Mosby. "Go ahead."

"Muerta was smart, all right, and salty," Hatfield resumed. "The notion of buying the Greasy Sack and hanging out, in disguise, right under the sheriff's nose, was a lulu. That way he could keep in touch with Dawson all the time, who was the real brains of the outfit, and also get information of what was going on. Only a jigger with plenty of stiffening in his back woulda done it.

"Their allus seeming to know what was going on also got me to thinking about Dawson," Hatfield resumed. "They knew just where to look for the Silver City cleanup, even though it was s'posed to have been sent to Alamita the day before. They found out about the big money shipment on the Sunset Flyer, and things like that. Dawson, being in the bank, had access to such information. I was sure of him when the conveyor line was robbed. Letting the cat outa the bag lay between him and Henry Blaine, and I never gave Blaine credit for much of anything. He was just the handy man for the bunch.

"Dawson was different. He had big notions, and came mighty nigh to putting them over. He was of the filibustering type, like William Walker, Crabbe, and old Sam Houston. Only he was different from them in that he was an owlhoot. Trace him back and the chances are you'd find him mixed up in plenty of shady deals. Using Muerta, who was plenty smart in his own way, as a front, he figgered he'd be able to put over the revolution idea in Mexico. If that succeeded, he would be sitting purty. Dawson knew the time was ripe for just such a move."

He paused, his green eyes inscrutable. "It is," he added quietly, "and before long it will come, but Dawson wasn't the man."

"He didn't end up bein' the man," Sheriff Wilson corrected. "I've a notion if it wasn't for you, Hatfield, he might have been, and it woulda been a mighty bad thing for Texas. Yuh did a mighty good chore, and did it in gen'wine Ranger style."

Old John Mosby coughed self-consciously. "I wanta put in a word here," he remarked. "I usta have a sorta pore opinion of the Rangers—sorta stems from Wade wantin' to be one when I didn't want him to be, I've a notion. I've plumb changed that opinion of late. Was goin' to help have a bill interduced in the next legislature meetin' to abolish the outfit. I've changed my mind. I'm goin' to have a bill interduced to increase their appropriation."

He turned to his son.

"And if yuh're still in the notion of jinin' up with 'em, I ain't no objections to offer," he added.

Wade Mosby looked startled, but it was Hatfield who spoke, smiling and shaking his head.

"Reckon not," he said. "Ranger work isn't exactly a chore for a marrying man. Figger Wade had better stick on here, John, and help yuh run yore business, so he can be home of nights."

Wade Mosby, with a glance at Helen, who

blushed rosy red under his regard, nodded emphatic agreement.

Hatfield stood up. He stretched his long arms above his head and smiled down at the group from his great height.

"Well, folks, reckon I'll be leavin'," he said. "Got another mite of a chore to do for Captain Bill."

Sheriff Wilson chuckled. "Which calls to mind a gabfest you and me had a while back. I reckon it *will be* sorta peaceful and quiet again after yuh're gone, only different from the way I meant it when I said it."

They watched him ride away, tall and graceful atop his great golden horse, a light of pleased anticipation in his strangely colored eyes, to where duty called and new adventure waited.

Center Point Large Print
600 Brooks Road / PO Box 1
Thorndike, ME 04986-0001 USA

(207) 568-3717

US & Canada:
1 800 929-9108
www.centerpointlargeprint.com